DANCES WITH
SHARKS

DANCES WITH
SHARKS

Dave Ames

Lodge
Pole
Press

Elliston, Montana

Typeset in Century Schoolbook by Melissa Brown, Helena, Montana

Cover Illustration by Biff Karlyn, Helena, Montana

Jacket Design by Melissa Brown and Jeff Schuller, Helena, Montana

10 9 8 7 6 5 4 3 2 1

First Printing

Printed in the United States of America

Published by Lodgepole Press, Box 205, Elliston, MT, 59728

ISBN 0-9770838-0-2

Library of Congress Catalog Number   2005907316

Nature, Travel, Fishing

CONTENTS

Disclaimer

A lot of people ask me whether my stories are true. The answer is kind of but not really. Most of the people are made up, and some of the places don't exist, but other than that it's all true as best I remember. These stories are meant to entertain as well as inform, and the scientific and historical information presented in this book should be used only as a wedge to open the door to further research.

ACKNOWLEDGEMENTS

Portions of the stories in this book were previously published under the following titles in the following publications:

"The Jaguar God," *Hooked on the Outdoors Magazine*

"The Good Old Days," *Fly Fisherman Magazine*

"Wildlife Casting," *The Drake Magazine*

"The Missing Gink," *Big Sky Journal*

There are two kinds of editors, the kind that tell you what's right, and the kind that tell you what's wrong. You need them both, and I would like to thank my editors, Tom Harpole and John Bayorth. I would also like to thank Biff Karlyn for his distinctive cover art, Bergetta Hubbard for keeping me in line with the grammatical standards of the Chicago Manual of Style, and Melissa Brown and Jeff Schuller for their inspired book design and typesetting.

Most of all I would like to thank Elizabeth Rivard, because without her love, help, and constant flow of unending support this book would have been no more real than a dream.

THE JAGUAR GOD

My beard was crusted white with ice balls as I leaned a pair of cross-country skis against the board-and-batten fir siding of my house. Wind-blown drifts of snow had been piled up head high since Thanksgiving. It had been an eternity since anything different had happened, anything at all. The winter days came like frozen clones, identical in every regard.

Cabin fever is enough to make strong men weep. I was born on the winter solstice and came into the world kicking and screaming. It was cold out there. I should have been born in flip-flops, not mukluks, and I was mired in a rut as deep as time as I scraped frost off the thermometer.

"Eight below zero," said the tiny red stub of mercury at the bottom the column.

"And that's as warm as it got today," I replied.

"Pretty damn cold," we agreed.

It's one thing to talk to inanimate objects: it's worse when they talk back. Dark clouds weighed heavy in the

1

long procession of storms that had been settling down from the continental divide since noon. By four the sky was black like the inside of a colon as I stripped off layer after layer of sweat-soaked polypropylene and stepped onto the bathroom scale.

"Finally," I said, "A diet that works."

"Yeah, baby," said the scale.

I'd always been skinny, all my life, and then came the dreary morning that the naked guy who was me in the mirror had no hips. The only skinny part was my legs. Twenty pounds more and I'd look like an egg on toothpicks, which wouldn't make dating any easier.

Something had to be done, so I bought a scale. Some sort of a diet was in order, but I was honest with myself.

"A diet can't involve willpower," we agreed.

The diet had to include cuisine I liked minus huckleberry fudge cheesecake. It had to be easy to follow, which meant limiting allowable foodstuffs. Success: in just four weeks I'd already lost twelve pounds on the revolutionary Red Wine and Oatmeal Diet.

The Red Wine and Oatmeal Diet is simple. Wine and oats, that's all you get, except for coffee. Containing domestic blends of both fiber and alcohol, it's a diet that keeps you feeling good at both ends.

Maybe a little too good at the bottom end. In the age of low-flush toilets there is such a thing as too much fiber. After basking in a steaming shower, I dressed in yesterday's clothes, and wandered toward another dinner for one. It feels good to lose weight, and standing at the kitchen sink, tapping my toes inside wool socks to the beat of Bob Marley, I mistook the delirium of cabin fever for a hot flash of inspiration.

Tonight, things would be different.

Tonight, instead of a bowl of oatmeal and a glass of wine, I'd have a bowl of wine and a glass of oatmeal. A hearty bowl of precocious Chianti; a heaping glass of stone-cut oats.

And later, perhaps a Mounds bar from the dessert tray.

Drinking wine out of a bowl takes both hands, so when the phone rang I squeezed the receiver to my ear with my shoulder and said:

"Hello?"

"How you'se doin'?"

Kids who grew up in New York City between the World Wars don't talk, they tawk, and the richly accented baritone voice in the receiver was unmistakable.

"Mercury," I said, pleasantly surprised.

"What's that slurping sound?" he asked.

Just because somebody has an idea doesn't necessarily mean it's a good one, as I looked down at a purple stain spreading like an octopus across the chest of a shirt I'd been planning on washing pretty soon anyway.

"There's a reason more people don't drink from bowls," I replied.

"I don't wanna know," said Mercury.

He was born *Mercurio Salvatore*, but became Mercury when his parents emigrated from Italy (*Mercurio* was no kind of name for an American kid). The name is apt, because even pushing seventy Mercury still bubbles with energy and enthusiasm for life. Grey-haired Mercury is as smart as the streets, and always has a deal or two cooking.

"What's up?" I asked.

"How would you'se like two weeks of bonefishing in Ascension Bay?" he asked. "I have a lodge all lined up."

Ascension Bay juts up into the Mexican Yucatan Peninsula. I'd been there once, twenty years earlier. It was a place I always thought I'd get back to, but never had.

"I'd like it a lot," I said. "But I just spent all my money getting my truck fixed."

"The trip is gratis," said Mercury. "Airfare, lodging, fishing, food, it won't cost you a dime."

If something sounds too good to be true, it generally is.

"What's the catch?" I asked.

"Even booze," said Mercury. "It's all on the house."

It was clear they knew nothing about me.

"Really," I said.

"Forget about it," said Mercury. "We go down to a fishing lodge, they take care of us, we take care of them, we use their boats, you teach a bunch of Mayan Indians how to be bonefishing guides is all."

I've been a fishing guide for twenty years. Guiding is my craft. Already I could think of a dozen things I wanted to tell those Mayans about what makes a good guide great. But what I knew best was trout, not bonefish. At best it would be a far stretch.

"The catch?" continued Mercury. "You have to do the whole class in Spanish."

Now that would be a real stretch. Most of my Spanish I learned from comic books between beers on the beach.

"Can you do it?" said Mercury. "It's kinda sudden."

"How sudden?" I asked.

"Next week sudden," he replied.

Hindsight was clear on this one. My travels over the years had shown that usually I had just enough Spanish to get myself in trouble. On the other hand, the window was rimed with a half inch of hoary white frost. Outside, it was so cold even the moose were bedded down.

"Can I do it?" I replied. "*Sí, señor.*"

I promised Mercury I'd e-mail him at least a basic class outline within the next couple days, then hung up the phone and turned to the dessert tray.

"Time for a celebration," I said.

The plate of candy bars was as happy as I was.

"Have two," it replied.

Smells can trigger the strongest of human memories, and the whiff of coconut in the Mounds bar had me flat on my back with stomach cramps on a Mayan beach just down the coast from where Mercury and I were soon headed. My body was in Montana, but my mind was in the land of coconut milk and honey, and I was thinking it was twenty years almost to the day since I'd last been in the Yucatan.

It was my first big road trip, ten thousand miles round-trip, from Montana to Belize and back in a Subaru station wagon named Sue. We were traveling on a shoestring, camping mostly, and the less we spent, the longer we could stay. Rum and coconut milk was the cheapest drink going; what I had yet to learn is that coconuts have medicinal properties.

Coconut meat acts as a laxative but coconut milk works more like a cork. It constipates you. A coconut milk cocktail can help plug you up if you've ingested bad water and have a bus to catch; a steady diet of coconut milk can make you feel as if a homeless person has taken up residence in your guts.

That's how I felt that day, laying on a towel in the hot sand at *Playa del Carmen*, sipping my coconut milk drink and reading a Mexican comic book with the aid of a Spanish-English dictionary. A hundred yards down the beach, a brightly colored mélange of tourists and locals stood in a ragged line to board the ferry that ran twice a day out to the island of *Cozumel*.

Cozumel is a scuba diver's paradise and also where the Spaniards first set foot in what is now Mexico. *Cortes the Conquistador* arrived in 1519 with five hundred men, sixteen horses, and ten sailing galleons he hoped to fill with treasure for his boss, the Catholic Queen of Spain.

At the time, seven million Native Americans lived in relative luxury in elaborate cities complete with temples, running water, and sacrificial virgins to appease their blood-thirsty Gods. The Spaniards were outnumbered four-teen-thousand-to-one and should have been easy pickings, but *Cortes* had smallpox in his pocket and an Aztec legend at his side. The Aztecs, a brown-skinned people, believed that their God, *Quetzacoatl*, would return as a white man.

The Spaniard, *Cortes*, in his pointy leather military hat, fit the bill. A common denominator of earthly religion is that Gods, when they visit, tend to show more wrath than mercy, so *Moctezuma*, the supreme Aztec ruler at the time, did what you do with Gods. He left an offering.

Moctezuma tried to bribe the White God into leaving by presenting Him with lavish gifts of royal treasure. It's how you treat Gods, hoping they'll take the money and run, but it was poor strategy on Spaniards.

"Spaniards," *Cortes* reputedly said, "Are troubled with a disease of the heart for which gold is a specific remedy."

By the time *Moctezuma* branded *Cortez* as a fraud it was already too late. Aztec princes who resented *Moctezuma's* rule befriended the Spaniards in yet another in a long line of plots to topple the empire. The intrigue worked, too well. Over the next century five million Native Americans died, mostly from the ravages of smallpox and other European diseases.

Moctezuma is gone but not forgotten. He now takes his revenge on foreign visitors in the form of a disease of the bowels for which coconut milk is a specific cure, and we all know what too much coconut milk can do.

Laying on the beach, I'd just turned a page in my comic book when the homeless person in my belly lashed out.

After six days without the urge to go the feeling was over-whelming. I folded up on my towel, knees to nose, groaning as I fought back the smooth muscle surge that racked my intestines.

Baño (bahn-yo) means bathroom, and a hundred yards down the beach a crudely lettered sign at the edge of the palm jungle advertised just such a sanctuary. It was the only structure on that part of the beach, a rickety shack built with weathered boards salvaged from the sea and tied together with jute twine.

I rolled to my feet and started moving. No way would I make it, not waddling like a duck with clenched cheeks. I began to run, but nobody runs in Mexico. It's too hot.

Startled sunbathers turned on their bright blankets to watch. Willpower alone stood between me and the ulti-mate embarrassment as I slammed the stick *baño* door shut on its leather hinges behind me while yanking down my shorts and dropping to the white porcelain toilet—all in one motion.

There was no seat, so I climbed back up out of the bowl, and braced myself with my hands. Chartreuse lizards scam-pered up and down the walls. The ventilation was excel-lent, since there was no ceiling, and when the time came I discovered the *baño* was missing more than just a roof.

Not only was there no toilet paper, there was no way to flush. The toilet didn't have a handle. It didn't even have a tank. It was just an empty bowl without a seat plopped down on the sand, except now it wasn't empty anymore.

The damnable brown skyscraper was more temple than turd. It's like a family curse. My lower intestine isn't so much large as jumbo. Combine that with the fact that sci-ence may one day find in the binding properties of beans and coconut milk a viable structural alternative to con-crete, and you can see why I went in search of tools.

I threw open the door, thinking maybe I'd get a branch from the jungle to chop the monument into manageable chunks. A wiry old man with a machete in a leather holster half as long as his leg was waiting outside. A man of experience, he carried his own roll of toilet paper.

I searched for the words to describe the situation.

"*Grande . . . problema . . . ,*" I said.

Big problem seemed to sum it up, because when I tried to go around the man he stepped sideways and cut me off as he burst into a flurry of light-speed Spanish. I caught only one word: *dinero*. It means money, and the man wanted mine. That marked him for either a beggar or a thief, the machete he pulled out tipped the scales toward thief.

I smiled my biggest, whitest smile.

"*Con permiso,*" I said. "Excuse me."

I faked left and went right, but without a lot of teeth to weigh him down the old man was surprisingly quick. He was grim as he blocked the way. He held up all four fingers on the hand missing a thumb and, since he needed one more to make five, he held up the machete. He then rapped a blade that had been sharpened so many times it looked like a sword against a sign I hadn't noticed beside the door.

"Five cents," read the hand-scrawled symbols.

Five cents is five *pesos* and I finally got it. Talk about an entrepreneur. The old man wasn't shaking me down. He was running a pay toilet for the convenience of the people who congregated at the ferry terminal. In terms of value given and received, five *pesos* didn't seem like nearly enough.

"Make it ten," I said.

I pulled thin worn coins from my pocket and gave the man what amounted to about thirty American cents. He in turn gave me the roll of toilet paper, which I handed back.

"*No gracias,*" I said. "Better that I swim."

The old man's eyes widened as I stepped aside and he got a first look at the job ahead. A while later I saw him filling a rusty bucket at the blue ocean, twenty years after that the empty beach at *Playa del Carmen* had boomed into a small city.

The only recognizable landmarks were the ocean and the ferry boat landing when Mercury and I arrived. The single *baño* on the beach had been replaced with a solid adobe wall of expensive oceanfront restaurants and beach volleyball arenas. The jungle had been paved with a thicket of kiosks, shops and bakeries that extended in a cacophony of hawking barkers as far as the ear could hear.

The idyllic Yucatan I remembered was gone. This was more Spanish Disneyland than Mexico. I feared I had returned too late, but bad roads make for good places, and the rutted track south into Ascension Bay was barely passable, just as it had always been.

The road is cut at and below sea level along a narrow spit of barrier sand that juts a hundred kilometers into the Gulf of Mexico. Pass through a soldiered checkpoint a quarter of the way down the peninsula and you're in the biosphere preserve called *Sian Kaan*, which in the Mayan language means "Where the Sky is born." Keep going nearly to the end of the spit and you'll come to a fancy fishing lodge, which is where panic was born when I stood for the first time as *el professor* in front of a bunch of stone-faced Mayan Indians.

The classroom was a rounded corner in the Taj Mahal of palm-thatched *palapas*, a cone-shaped masterpiece sixty feet in diameter and thirty feet high at the central peak. A mere hundred feet of white sand separated me from the coral blue ocean, gentle waves lapped on the beach. It was only nine in the morning but already my shirt was soaked with enough sweat to drip onto the raised teak and mahogany floor.

"*Hola*," I said. "Hello."

Nine Mayans sat in a semicircle of wooden chairs before me. Every head was down, each squat man intently studying his own gnarled brown toes as I launched into one of a few lines of Spanish I'd had time to actually practice.

"This week," I said. "I hope that I learn the same from you as you learn from me."

Not one Mayan Indian so much as raised a bristling black eyebrow. They could have been carved from wrinkled brown wood. I waved my hands back and forth hoping to convey the two-way passage of information.

"*Bueno*," I said, "I hope we learn from us. *Bueno*. Together. Both. *Bueno*."

Bueno means good but is also used like the American "and uh," as filler for dead space while your brain searches for the next word. But so far it wasn't good at all.

Nobody had even moved yet.

"A guide," I said, "Has to be captain of his own boat."

Rich or famous clients can be intimidating. I saw in the head-down Mayans a familiar posture of inferiority induced by generations of discrimination, just as you see on the Blackfoot Reservation in Montana. I wanted to say that a guide has to take charge. I wanted to say that it doesn't matter how much money a man has, because in a boat on the ocean, everybody is equal.

"When you first meet your clients at the boat in the morning," I tried to say, "It's important to shake their hands and look them in the eye."

It was too much too soon for my pidgin Spanish. As soon as the words left my mouth I realized I'd used nose for hand and probably switched subjects beside, which meant I'd just said something like: "Before encountering your rich fishermen in the morning, rub them with your eyes and look up their noses."

I knew I'd said it badly because the Mayans finally moved. They exchanged sidelong glances through the salt-weathered creases at the edge of their dark eyes, and then went back to studying the floor at their feet through corrugated faces as ageless and expressionless as bark.

I'd been thinking it had been too long since I'd been to the Yucatan, now I was thinking I never should have come back. What could I, a *gringo*, hope to teach these Indians about fishing? The Mayans had been hauling bonefish out of these flats for thousands and thousands of years.

For century after century, while Europe remained mired in the Dark Ages, the Mayans ruled over a highly advanced civilization. Mayan city-states, housing up to a quarter million people, and complete with roads, aqueducts, temples, trade, and three systems of writing, speckled Central America. Mathematics was a Mayan specialty. The Mayans were among the first people to come up with the concept of zero, which opened the floodgates on a slew of mathematical breakthroughs, particularly in the area of astronomy.

Mayan arithmetic was very simple. Dots were worth one, bars were worth five, and a figure that looks like a smiling seashell denoted a zero. With only those three symbols Mayan Jaguar priests calculated the movements of the universe. The priests precisely predicted astrological events three thousand years into their future, and devised a complicated dual calendar so precise it was one-thousandth of a day more accurate than the one we use today.

The Mayans used two calendars because for them time didn't run in straight lines, it ran in spirals. They deduced from their astronomical observations that time comes and goes in recurring cycles of creation and destruction dictated by the stars to last exactly fifty-two hundred years. According to Mayan reckoning, the current age and world as we know it is supposed to end in A.D. 2011 or 2012.

As far as my students were concerned the Mayan apocalypse couldn't come soon enough. They were so intent on their feet that all they showed of their heads was the scruff of their necks. The class hadn't even decently begun and already it was slipping away as I picked up a black magic marker and turned to the sheaf of white presentation paper hanging from a rusty nail on the palm-thatched wall. A big yellow spider with brown hairy legs emerged from the palm fronds and raced the squeaking black magic marker across the paper in the stark humid silence as I wrote in big block letters:

"*LA PROPINA.*"

La Propina rhymes with Gina and means "The Tip." Cash on the barrel head is universal guide language. The spider crawled back into the wall, taking its time. When I couldn't put it off any longer I turned around; a wide Mayan in a red Def Leppard T-shirt was elbowing a skinny Mayan beside him and pointing at what I'd written.

"The tip most big that I receive for one day guiding," I said, "Is one thousand dollars."

In rural Mexico, that's more than most people make in a year. One by one, the class looked up. I let the sentence hang until eighteen dark eyes were trained my way.

"For to be a good guide," I continued, "There are three things you have to know."

I turned back to the paper and in more big block letters wrote the English word "SERVICE," along with its Spanish counterpart, the word "*SERVICIO.*"

"*Ser-vic-i-o*" rhymes with "hair-piece-ee-o," and a good guide can never forget that he is part of a service industry. You have to take care of your clients. You have to make them comfortable. Out on the water you're part butler, caterer, counselor, storyteller, and navigator. You're everything it takes to bring people home not just alive, but smiling.

"*Servicio,*" I said. "Very important. Service."

I had them repeat after me in both languages. At the very least I figured I could teach them English.

"*Servicio, servicio, servicio,*" we said together.

"Service, service, service."

Mercury stood up and rubbed his fingers together in the international signal for money.

"Soivice," he said, "Soivice, soivice, soivice."

"Soivice," repeated the class in passable Brooklynese.

I mopped my brow as Mercury distributed our first bribes. Each student received a clipboard, a yellow legal pad, and a couple of pencils with which to take notes. Something I hoped for each student to compile during the class was a Spanish-English dictionary of fishing terms, and I pointed at the sheath of presentation paper.

"*Escribelo,*" I said, "Write it down."

Each student diligently wrote in his notebook at a different speed. When they were mostly done I wrote out the second rule of good guiding, then we said it out loud.

"*Planear, planear, planear.*"

"Plan, plan, plan."

It's not enough to find fish once in a while over the course of a day. Good guides find fish consistently over an eight hour period, which requires an informed plan that factors in daily variables such as tides, weather, angler ability, and crowds. Every morning you have to think about the journey ahead and come up with a plan to produce the daunting miracle of fish on demand.

"Rule number three," I said, "And most important . . ."

In the biggest letters yet I wrote:

"*Enseñar, enseñar enseñar.* Teach, teach, teach."

The ability to teach is what separates the great guides from the good guides because once you find fish, you have to teach the clients how to catch them. That's what makes the legends, the guides who always get fish. They're teachers.

The essence of teaching is to understand something so well that you can explain it in a number of different ways. No way can you teach something if you can't do it yourself.

Demonstration is a key teaching aid.

"And because of this," I finished, groping for words, "There is no graduation before catching a bonefish with a fly of your own . . . your own . . . "

I straggled to a stop, searching for the Spanish verb "to tie." The students looked around the room, sizing up the competition. Even though I'd run out of linguistic gas they knew what I meant. Nobody graduated until they caught a fish on a fly they'd tied themselves, and a Mayan with a gold chain around his neck twisted his stubby fingers around an imaginary knot.

"*Atar*," he said. "Toot-eye."

The accent was heavy but it was English. "To tie," he was saying, and our Spanish-English dictionary of fishing terms was now richer by another important word.

"*Gracias*," I said.

"*Repitelo*," he said. "Ree-peed eet."

He was telling me to repeat it, parodying what I'd been doing all morning, and it got a laugh from the class.

"*¿Como se llama?*" I asked him. "What's your name?"

The Mayan could have been thirty or he could have been sixty. I just couldn't tell as he drew a deep breath into his barrel chest then looked off toward the round Mayan calendar of carved mahogany that hung on the wall behind me.

"*Pato*," he replied.

Pato means Duck, and I asked him where he'd learned his English.

"Atlanta," he replied.

Pato, in a fine blend of Spanglish, told me he'd been sent by the Mexican government on an all expenses paid trip to America to learn the English of ecotourism, except he pronounced it tour-eesm.

"Tour-ism," I corrected. *"Repitelo."*

"Tour-eesm," repeated the class.

A big difference between Spanish and English is the way vowels are pronounced. The Spanish *"e"* sounds like the English "a," the Spanish *"i"* sounds like the English "e," and the soft English "i" of "fish" or "it," for all practical purposes, doesn't even exist in the Spanish language.

"Fish," I said. *"Repitelo."*

"Feesh," they repeated.

Mercury leapt up and used his hands to show the vowels moving away from his mouth.

"I-i-i," he said, drawing out the sound of the soft "I," "Fi-i-i-ish."

"Ee-e-e," repeated the Mayans. "Fe-e-esh."

Language circuits are wired into the brain at an early age. If you don't have it, it isn't there. Learning a new sound is tough. It takes repetition, until the new information is stuck so deeply into the brain that it sets up its own system of communication with the outside world.

Guiding also requires repetition, and repetition requires patience. You'll show somebody how to set the hook a dozen times before they get it right. Then you'll start all over again tomorrow, a dozen more times, and you can't ever show frustration no matter how you feel.

"The three rules of guiding," I said. "What are they?"

Writing is a benchmark development in the history of humanity because it allows people to remember what they have forgotten. Writing is like having another brain, and the Mayans looked down at their yellow pads.

"¿*Enseñar?*" said an older looking guy with a lined face and three gold teeth that gleamed as he smiled.

"¿*Planear?*" said a couple of students together.

"Sur-veece?" said *Pato*, tentatively trying his English.

Mercury threw his hands straight up toward the roof of the *palapa* like somebody had scored a touchdown.

"Now you're tawking," he said.

The one skill every fly-fishing guide teaches every day is proper casting technique, and our goal was to give Spanish speaking Mayans the ability to teach casting to English speaking clients. It's best to begin even the most complex job with the basics, so I turned to a fresh sheet of paper and drew a vertical black line down the middle of the page.

"*Caña*," I said. "Rod."

I wrote, they wrote. We practiced the words in both languages, then I drew a circle at the bottom of the black line.

"*Carretera*," I said, "Reel."

The bilingual diagram on the white paper grew item by item; line, leader, loop, tippet, fly. Then we learned some verbs, enough to form simple sentences that distilled the physics of casting down to the essential golden rules.

"*Flojo es malvado*," I said. "Slack is evil."

You can't cast slack, period.

"To make a cast," I said, "Bend the rod."

Fly rods are expensive because of the way in which they bend when you wave them back and forth. The idea during a cast is to get the energy that's stored in the bent rod to transfer into the fly line, and the more energy that is transferred the better the cast will be.

"The loop," I said. "It's all about the loop."

The same principle that cracks a bullwhip propels a fly line. It's called the Law of Conservation of Angular Momentum, and part of what the Law means is that a loop as it uncoils transfers energy to the line from which it's formed.

"To form a loop," I said, "Stop the rod."

A cast is an acceleration of the rod through an arc to an abrupt stop, and it is the stop that transfers the energy from the bend in the rod to the loop in the line. A sharp stop transfers power; a sloppy stop doesn't. It's a critical point and I used my arm to demonstrate.

"Stop the rod," I said. "You have to stop it."

Mercury reaffirmed what I had to say with vigorous karate chops into the open palm of his other hand.

"Stawp the rod," he exclaimed. "Stawp it! Stawp it!"

The resounding slap of Mercury's karate chops drove scurrying green chameleons into hiding behind the glass goblets on the shelf behind the tiki bar that beckoned from beside the lounge we were using as a classroom.

"Stawp eet," repeated the students.

It's tough teaching casting even if you speak the same language, and after a day of concentrating in Spanish my brain was exhausted. I wondered if I'd been exposed for the charlatan that I was. My greatest worry was that no students would return for the second day of class. I'd have to pay for my own plane ticket home, and it was cold back home. So, in the heat of the afternoon, I dismissed the class with that most delicate of Mexican traditions, *la mordida*.

La mordida translates as "the bite," but it's also "the bribe," an institution that greases the wheels of Mexican society at every level. At its most basic *la mordida* is the bite of the few *pesos* a traffic cop demands to ignore alleged traffic violations; it's also the ten percent kickback top government officials routinely divvy up in the aftermath of a billion dollar oil deal.

When bribing, certain formalities must be observed. You have to be discrete, a lesson I learned my first five minutes in Mexico. I was driving into the country, had heard that customs officials expected to be bribed, and was thus prepared with a five dollar bill as I finally arrived at the head of a line of traffic backed up a quarter mile at the border crossing. An orange wooden arm that swung up and down was all that separated me from Mexico as a fat man in an army uniform put his arms on the window sill beside my head.

"*Señor*," he said in thickly accented English. "For how long you being in Mexico?"

"Six months," I said. "It's a fishing trip."

The border guard shook his head as if he was sad.

"Six months," he said, "But I am afraid that cannot be arranged."

The concrete compound surrounding me was a pandemonium of honking horns and vendors screaming in a cloud of blue exhaust. The border guard's brown face smelled like it had been dipped in sweet cologne as he leaned through the window.

"Will this help?" I asked.

I pulled out the five dollar bill and waved it around; the guard's thin eyebrows rose over his mirrored sunglasses.

"You will come with me," he said sternly. "Now."

I pulled out the other five I had ready just in case.

"*Señor*," I said, "Perhaps . . ."

I could tell by his expression that I'd blown it. A rusted pick-up truck full of live chickens in wire cages belched black smoke and backfired in the next entrance lane over as the guard reached inside and opened my car door.

"Come with me," he commanded. "*Ahorito*."

I followed him through a wooden door into a windowless concrete room furnished with a concrete bench and what looked like dried blood on the floor. The guard stuck out his hand and I braced myself for a punch but he merely put a finger to my lips.

"Sh-h-h," he said, and then pointed at the money I'd stuck in my pocket.

"Sh-h-h."

Honor is all important in Mexico and I'd unknowingly insulted the man. It wasn't that he didn't want the bribe, it's just that I was too obvious, and the guard looked into the space to the left of my head.

"It is said that it is difficult to live on the salary of a government official," he said.

"I have heard that same thing," I replied, cautiously.

The guard smiled pleasantly, in no hurry now that we were cloaked in the secrecy of concrete. The hint seemed clear and I pulled one of the five dollar bills from my pocket.

"Perhaps this would help with the difficulties," I said.

The guard took the five in my hand, and then reached for my pocket and snaked out the other five.

"Help is good," he said, "But more help is better."

Honor was preserved because it's true. Policemen don't receive decent salaries. They rely on bribes to survive by trumping up traffic charges, and then taking a little bite to look the other way. At higher levels *la mordida* takes the form of kickbacks. You can get things done in Mexico, but it's going to cost you, usually ten to fifteen percent.

As an example, suppose you want to sell the police a thirty thousand dollar car. Figure in ten percent or three thousand dollars for whoever signs off on the deal; then, charge thirty-three thousand for the car to cover the cost of doing business. It's a sweetheart deal and everybody's happy, except that goods cost more than they're worth.

Inflation is built into the system, and ten percent adds up to long-term economic instability when applied on a grand scale to businesses like *Pemex*, the Mexican equivalent of Big Oil. *La mordida* allows Mexican presidents and their henchmen to live in opulent mansions, it also ensures *Pemex* of pricing difficulties when competing in a global market.

Bribes are the grease that spin the wheels of Mexican society, and in our attempt to get the class to return for a second day, Mercury and I had come prepared. The students elbowed and nudged each other as Mercury slit open a long cardboard box to reveal the slim graphite prizes within.

"*Mañana*," I said, "Your own rod of fishing."

Mercury, a first-rate wheeler-dealer, had arranged for the use of enough fly rods and reels to put a complete outfit in every Mayan's hand. It couldn't have happened without the generosity of the conservation-oriented Orvis Company, and I was seeking the words to give thanks for environmentally proactive businesses when I hit the cortical wall.

"uhhh . . . , " I said.

My mouth was open but not one more word of Spanish would come out. The only thing I could produce was a little drool. My brain was totally fried shut but Mercury was smiling like he'd just had good chocolate.

"Class," he said, "Dis-missed."

Nine Mayan Indians trooped out looking like they didn't quite believe it. No sooner had they gone than *El Jefe*, the owner of the lodge, strolled up in his white Panama suit.

"Well," he said. "Well, well, well."

Mercury reached up and put a hand on my shoulder.

"I tole you," he said. "I tole you we could do it."

El Jefe (pronounced *Heff-fay*) means "The Boss," and he had a big cigar and creased hat to go with his linen suit.

"Do you have a name for your school?" he asked.

What I was thinking about was lesson plans. We'd gone through three lesson plans already and I'd only prepared four. You didn't have to be a Mayan mathematician to see where that was heading. Mentally I was just treading water so it was a while before I noticed *El Jefe* and Mercury staring at me.

"Huh?" I said.

"A name," said Mercury. "We gots to come up with a name."

What I needed more than a name was to taste the salt in the breeze, to let the sun soak my winter-bleached hide, to bury my toes in the sand. All day long, a hundred feet away, the ocean had been calling, and it was high time I answered.

"OK," I said. "I'm coming."

Mercury looked at *El Jefe* who looked worried as I picked up my fly rod from the rack by the *palapa* door.

"Forget about it," Mercury was saying as I left, "He just needs to go fishing is all. Now, about them boats . . ."

The tide line was marked with plastic bottles labeled in Spanish, English, and Japanese as I walked to the end of a mat of tangled brown kelp that had been squished long and flat against the beach by a week of north winds. Thirty feet out the ocean was clear cobalt blue, but the band of water along the surf-tossed shore was grey with roily sand.

I stood in the churning water so that the rising waves tugged at the hair on my thighs, then pasted the hair flat on my calves as they broke behind me. A white egret with yellow legs snatched a silver minnow from the kelp bed as I tried to become one with a rolling ocean full of squawking seagulls. I don't know how long I stood there with my eyes at half-mast, but when I finally looked up there were three permit rooting ten feet away at the edge of the kelp bed.

Permit!

Permit are the Holy Grail of saltwater flats fishing. Most times you fish days or maybe weeks for permit without even seeing one. Permit never just show up at your doorstep, especially not so close you can dap for them.

A rod length away, I lowered a weighted crab fly down to the permit in the weed-free water at the edge of the kelp bed. If something seems too good to be true it generally is. The next wave carried my fly past the fish and into the kelp, and there's no such thing as a little kelp.

Kelp survives as coherent beds in the storm-tossed seas because the knobby brown strands grow together like Velcro. I yanked, pulled, twisted, and poked my line. The permit had eyes as big as black-and-white donuts. They must have seen me, but the big round fish just kept feeding as I tried to remain invisible while releasing a thousand pound wad of weeds.

The kelp came apart one tendril at a time, and at few times in my life have I been as bitterly disappointed as when I finally freed my fly. I fought the seaweed, and the seaweed won. In the tussle I'd snapped my rod at the first ferrule, and no way could I land a permit on a rod butt.

I dropped to my belly and crawled past pitted buoys trailing frayed rope. I stood up and ran around a chunk of waterlogged plywood with corners that had been tumbled round in the surf. Mercury and *El Jefe* were sitting in chairs on the open deck at the main *palapa* as I chugged on by.

"See," said Mercury, "I told you he'd be all right."

I wanted to keep my mouth shut. The permit represented an opportunity I wanted to keep secret until I rigged another rod but it felt like bad juju. Mercury had let me in on his deal, it was only fair I let him in on mine.

"Permit," I gasped as I opened a rod case.

Mercury bounded to his stout bowed legs.

"Poim-it!" he said.

Italian curses rode the onshore breeze back to the *palapa* as I strung sky blue fly line through the chrome guides of my spare rod. Mercury, casting to the permit, wasn't having any more luck with the kelp than I'd had.

Think, I thought, *think.*

Conventional wisdom holds that bottom-feeding permit should be fished with weighted crab flies, but in the kelp a weighted fly wouldn't work. The fly would sink and I'd just get hung up again, but in the churning surf it seemed the permit might be eating anything knocked loose. It was at least possible the fish would be looking up for their meals.

What I needed was a floating crab, and since all my crabs were weighted, I spent five minutes at the house vice tying up a floating brown and green polypropylene crab with foam legs on a number two hook. Back at the beach, I arrived just in time to watch Mercury release a giant wad of kelp.

"Nice one," I said.

"Tanks," he replied.

Two of three permit were still there, but looking nervous as they drifted in and out of the deeper water.

"You want your spot back?" asked Mercury.

A trout fishing rule of thumb is that you never leave rising fish to find more rising fish. It was probably the same with permit, but Mercury was trembling with the need to cast.

"Keep it," I said. "I feel like going for a walk."

A half mile to the south more kelp had been pushed up against the shore. It was a good bet for more feeding permit, and I started down the beach scrutinizing the dirty water next to shore where the waves stirred up the food.

The surging brown seam rose and fell. Even the shadows had shadows beneath the churning waves, but only one shadow moved deliberately from left to right, coming toward me as it disappeared into a clump of kelp.

It had to be a permit, a whopper judging by the long shadow, and I dropped to a crouch on the tide washed sand. I was positioned at a relatively kelpless clearing in the muck, and when the shadow that moved with purpose reappeared I flipped out the floating crab.

Fifteen feet away, the drab crab was totally invisible on the surface of the brown water. A fish would never be able to see my fly in the midst of all the other flotsam. I had just enough time to have that thought when the shadow in the murk grew darker and much longer as it charged the fly.

When I felt the fish, I set the hook, pulling with the rod low and away. The cork handle shivered as sharp metal stuck solid meat. The line went tight to the sound of rattling scales as a four foot silver tarpon jumped five feet in the air, spinning hard enough to spray me with fishy-smelling water.

The tarpon jumped again, and again, soaking me each time, then took off for the deep blue sea. Tarpon scales and gill rakers are sharp as razors. To have a realistic chance at landing tarpon you need a thick piece of shock tippet at the end of your line, at least sixty pound monofilament.

I was rigged for selective permit with much lighter tippet, and the line broke on the next jump. When I caught up with Mercury I showed him the ragged cut where the tarpon had abraded through the leader.

"It was unbelievable," I said. "I thought it was a permit, then this tarpon erupts fifteen feet away."

Mercury waved his arms like he was trying to fly.

"Poimit and tarpon," he said. "All in the first hour of fishing. Unbelievable is right."

It's rare to find such good fishing so close to the lodge and I wondered what we'd find in the backcountry.

"I've never seen anything like it," I said.

"Wait til' you see the flats," said Mercury. "You'se gonna love this place."

"I already do," I said.

We talked fish talk as we walked back along the beach toward the lodge. The air was cooling with the evening, and I was feeling good, really good. This is when I generally drink too much alcohol, and *El Jefe* was a man after my own heart.

"*Margarita?*" he asked.

Standing at the tiki bar under the *palapa* on the beach, winter seemed so very, very far away.

"*Grande,*" I replied.

Mercury remembers World War II and held up the "V" for Victory sign.

"*Dos,*" he said.

The bar was a semicircle of polished ebony supported by carved bas-relief panels of Mayan Gods. The Gods were depicted in a variety of war like poses, and above their blunt wooden heads lush tropical fish swam through stained glass the color of the sea. The *margaritas* came in thick medieval goblets that took two fists to hold, and it wasn't long before I was staring up at the symmetrical ceiling.

It's easy to get lost in the structure of a good *palapa* because subtle harmonies underlie the fabric of the universe. Certain constants describe the way reality is constructed. The ancient Mayans didn't just know about these constants, they incorporated these magic numbers into the designs of their temples, homes, and cities.

Everybody's heard of pi, 3.14159 ad infinitum. Pi is an irrational number that just keeps going and going. Pi is the ratio of circumference to diameter of every circle in the universe, and that's a lot of circles. It's a constant.

Pi is fundamental to the way energy spreads in a circular plane. There's another universal constant, phi, which better describes living things. Plants and animals can only grow by the addition of cells, one cell at a time. When you add those cells at a rate and in such a manner that volume increases at a constant rate, that's phi.

Visually, phi is the spiral in a conch's shell. Numerically it's another never-ending number, 1.61803, and so on through the galaxies. Phi determines the whorl of seeds in a sunflower, the spacing of fins on a porpoise, the horizon in a Renaissance painting, the layout of the human face, the dimensions of a *palapa*, and it all starts with a line.

Take a line, any line.

Divide the line into two pieces of unequal length, so that the ratio of the short side to the long side equals the ratio of the long side to the whole original line. That's phi. It's also called the golden mean, and derives mathematically from the Fibonacci series; 1, 2, 3, 5, 8, 13, 21, 34, 55; the number series you get when you keep adding the last two numbers together. Divide any number in this sequence by the number before it, and that ratio gets ever closer to the universal constant phi. Confused? The Mayans weren't.

They laid out their temples to conform to the ratios of the golden mean using only a length of vine. To do it you start with a rectangle that is two lengths of the vine wide by three vine lengths long. Add two vine lengths to the long side, the new rectangle is five vines long by three vines wide. Add three vines to the five vines, the new rectangle is eight vines by five vines. Add eight to the five, the new rectangle is thirteen vines wide and eight vines long.

Wow.

The Mayans lived in tune with their environment like few civilizations before or since. The basic everyday *palapas* in which people cooked, cleaned, and copulated were built to the ratios of the Golden Mean as a constant reminder that people live in spirals like flowers grow. The elegantly simple *palapa*, a stick-framed shelter thatched with a palm hip roof, is a design so suited to the climate that it's still in use after fifty centuries of fishermen living on this beach.

  As for me, I definitely remember feeling like I was one with the universe at the tiki bar in the Taj Mahal of all *palapas*. The next thing I definitely remember is waking up foggy the next morning, naked between clean sheets. Which was a pleasant surprise. A lot of places I wake up foggy and naked in Mexico there aren't even beds.

Tropical birds screamed in the morning dew as my body checked in. Stomach, mouth, and skull; nauseous, dry, and throbbing. On the next bed over Mercury sat up and scratched the grey pelt of chest hair above his white boxers.

"Can I akse you something?" he said.

Up above, the ceiling fan went around and around.

"Sure," I said.

"What did we have for dinner last night?"

I'd been about to ask him the same thing.

"I don't know," I said. "It was good though."

Mercury lay back down, not quite ready to face the day. Up above, the fan went around and around. I remembered eating, but for the life of me, I couldn't remember what we'd had for dinner, and I looked over at Mercury.

He was already looking at me.

"We shouldn't have had that second margarita," we said in exact unison.

La cruda rhymes with barracuda and feels like it sounds, crude. It's a hangover, the nausea deep into the spine of the desolate morning after. The ancient Mayans would have understood. They had Gods for both wine and tattoos, and of the nine levels they assigned to Underworld Hell, my stomach was still at about level five.

Fried eggs with black beans and bacon helped, but it was the brisk January wind off the ocean that really turned the trick. The bribe had worked. We were up to twelve students from nine, and twenty-four brown eyes followed Mercury's every move as he arranged fly-fishing tackle on the restaurant tables under the giant *palapa*.

"*Bueno*," I said, "Go for it."

When the limestone dust had settled each student hovered alongside a table covered with a white tablecloth and a complete fly-fishing outfit, some assembly required. In order to use their gear, they were going to have to put it together.

"*Nudos*," I said, "Knots."

Fishing guides use dozens of specialized knots but it's possible to do the job with a foundation of only four. We went over the arbor knot that ties the backing to the reel; the nail knot that ties the backing to the line and the leader to the line; the blood knot that ties the tippet to the leader; and the clinch knot that ties the fly to the tippet.

A fact of teaching is that students learn at different rates. Some students require more individual attention than others do. It was true of knot tying, and, out on the beach, it was even more true of casting.

Pato had the most trouble. He couldn't quite get the casting rhythm, but neither could he let it go. Mercury was working with *Pato*, and even though flailing green loops of fly-line were beginning to collapse about their ears, still *Pato* kept pumping away with the fly rod.

"Stawp!" yelled Mercury. "Stawp!"

Mercury clung to *Pato's* forearm, trying to incorporate the all-important stop into the casting motion, but *Pato* was too strong. Each full-length swing of *Pato's* arm was

accompanied by a sideways step for more full-body leverage, and Mercury's heels left furrows in the sand as he was
dragged back and forth like a plow.

"Stawp! Stawp the rod high!"

But *Pato* didn't stop, not until his arm was tied to his
neck. When it was safe again Mercury stepped back in,
smiled, and began to undo *Pato* from his trusses.

"Forget about it," said Mercury. "It could a happened to
anybody-oh."

Mercury was coming up with a language all his own, created by adding the hard Spanish "oh" to the end of English
words, like spaghettio is Spanish for spaghetti. It worked
because Mercury says more with body language than most
people manage with sonnets. Once *Pato* was freed Mercury
took the rod and arced back the tip in demonstration of the
first rule of casting.

"Bend-oh el rod-oh," he said, "That's what I axed you."

His hands sliced through the casting arc, stopping at
ten and two. When somebody got it right he'd jump up and
down with both hairy arms straight over his head. We went
from student to student, working with each one in turn to
the tune of wind-tossed snatches of salsa music that played
between the hiss of breaking waves.

The music came from a transistor radio propped up
against a coconut beside a pair of natural brunettes sharing the same bright blanket. Maybe the girls owned bath-
ing suits but you wouldn't know it from how they dressed.

Naked people just aren't something you see in Montana.
I had to stare, I was just trying not to get caught staring
as two armed soldiers clad in olive drab approached the
class from the north. The soldiers walked the litter strewn
strand line of the beach, their polished black high-lace
boots kicking through the kelp and plastic bottles.

The vast wilderness of Ascension Bay is a wayfaring point on the Colombia to Miami drug smuggling route. Deals go sour out there on the ocean. Merchandise gets lost. Mexican soldiers patrol the shoreline constantly searching for the watertight bales and airtight suitcases that help fund the army when they wash in on the tide.

These two soldiers, when they came to the line of casting Mayans, kept walking. The soldiers didn't go around the class; they didn't change their stoic expressions. The soldiers just kept marching straight down the gauntlet of furling and unfurling lines, like we weren't even there.

The Mayans, for their part, kept throwing loops, like they hadn't noticed that if they dropped their back cast they might snag a submachine gun. The Mayans didn't stop casting and allow the soldiers to pass because it would have showed weakness. As for the soldiers, no way could they change their path to accommodate the casting Mayans.

It was a situation as Mexican as it gets because honor was at stake. Nobody would yield because everybody had the right-of-way. The fly lines circled the soldiers but never touched in a visualization of the delicate and dynamic balance that so characterizes *machismo*.

It isn't easy being a *macho* man. For a glimpse at what it's like, try this theory on for Freudian size.

It all goes back five centuries to when your symbolic mother, a willowy Indian princess dressed in feathers, was raped by your symbolic father, a squat little *conquistador* with a bad complexion, shiny armor, and a pointy leather hat. If you're a male child of that union it's a tough heritage to reconcile, because deep down you feel like your mother let you down. Her native culture wasn't enough to ward off the Spaniards, so you feel a little shame at your ancestry.

Plus, your father can't trust your mother. Not after what he's done. A jade knife in the back, that's what your father deserves, but still, he's flesh and blood. He can't be all bad, and if your father can't trust your mother, then how can you possibly trust your own wife?

The *macho* answer is that you can't.

A tenet of *machismo* is that you believe you will be betrayed by women. It's just the way girls are, and to some extent it's a self-fulfilling prophecy. If you act like an asshole long enough, then your masculinity will be challenged. If you believe you will be betrayed, then you will be betrayed, and since you knew all along that your wife couldn't be trusted, there's one surefire way to prove your virility.

Take a girlfriend.

It's called *la casa chica*, the little house, but it means a girlfriend on the side. The double life carries with it a heaping helping of guilt, a situation exacerbated by the fact that from your symbolic Spanish father you inherited the religion of Catholicism, and nobody does guilt like the Catholics.

As a *macho* man, it's all your fault.

You hadn't even been born yet, but you'd failed to protect your mother from the raping *conquistadors*. You'd failed to protect your nation. Five centuries of accumulated guilt is a mighty load to carry. So you have to prove yourself. All the time. Which, of course, is impossible, and when you've had so much of failure that you can't stand it any longer; well, then it's time to drown the guilt in ritual drinking.

Ritual drinking is nothing at all like having a couple of beers after work. There is a terrible desperation to the act and it strikes hardest at indigenous populations. Take your average guy, a father and provider, a good country man. He hasn't had a drink in years, suddenly he bursts. The binge will last for days, weeks, or months, depending on how much money is available.

Later that afternoon, by the looks of it, the gang of Mayans drinking in the shade of the thatched roof at the end of the boat dock had plenty of money available. Beer cans and half-awake bodies littered the plank floor and benches as *Pato* and I arrived to gas up the boats for an afternoon of fishing.

Empty cans rattled as the wind blew them about, a few beers but no visible corpses floated out with the tide. Out of five Mayans only one man was standing, and if he had Spanish blood running through his veins it wasn't obvious. Four-and-a-half feet tall, four-and-a-half feet wide, with a chest like a Volkswagen; he had a wide flat nose with flared nostrils and gnarled toes that looked prehensile enough to crack walnuts.

"Fucking *gringo*," he said.

It's stupid to take the bait but defending your honor isn't just a Latin thing, it's a male thing. The man's blood-shot corneas were watermelon red around his black pupils, and I stared right back with my own red and blue eyes for a while before I turned to *Pato*.

"Who it this is?" I said.

Pato was pushing a wheelbarrow full of plastic gasoline containers, and he looked away as he rubbed at the splin-tered dock with his square brown toe.

"*Chac*," he muttered.

"¿*El Guía*?" I said in surprise.

"*Sí*," said *Pato*.

"Fucking *gringo*," said *Chac* again.

Guía means "guide," and by all reports *Chac* was the best guide around. I guessed his age at forty but he could have been sixty. He got fish when nobody else could, lots of them, so many he'd been nick-named after *Chac Uayab Xoc*, the Mayan God of Fishing.

All Mayan Gods have dual natures, a *yin* and a *yang*, and *Chac Uayab Xoc* in the pictures on temple walls was generally depicted as a shark. Think about it. You're out there, alone in the ocean. Your dugout canoe is swamped, the sail blown away, the squat mast broken. You're out of drinking water, the end is near, and for help you pray to the Shark God.

That's a tough culture.

The Shark God ate drowned fishermen, but he also provided good catches. Nature was cruel, but nature was bountiful. Even today freebies sometimes wash up on the tide. The soldiers don't get it all, and the word on the beach was that while guiding one day *Chac* found more than just fish.

He hadn't shown up for work in over two months, but every binge has its end. *Chac* knew the day would come when he'd need his job back. He wouldn't teach the new guides the tricks of the trade, because when he did come back, he didn't want competition. I was there to teach the students what he wouldn't, and now *Chac* looked past me toward *Pato*.

"Only stupid pubic hairs," said *Chac*. "Would need a lizard-licking *gringo* to teach them what has been known to their fathers since before the temples fell."

The gutter Spanish was right up my comic book alley. If you have money you'll have friends and *Chac's* cronies, those of them who were still awake, laughed appreciatively. Emboldened, *Chac* threw up his square brown hands.

"The illegitimate sons of male goat Americans," he said, "They come where they are not welcome. You are no better than your dog-piss president who is not a president."

The average *Latino* is far better informed about current world events than the average American because Uncle Sam has a long history of interfering in Latin America. For instance, the CIA in 1954 sponsored a coup to support the

United Fruit Company that led to a civil war in which over two million people were killed. In another instance, United States-backed contras in El Salvador devastated Nicaragua in the 1980s because an Indian rights land movement was deemed Communistic. The list goes on and on; the more I learn, the more I'm amazed.

I can't count the times I've been pulled aside by a *campesino* out in the middle of Mexican nowhere for an earnest discussion on the imperialistic particulars of American foreign policy. Much of what they told me I had to check out later because it was new to me. These country people kept up on current events. They talked to me like they thought I could make a difference, like votes really counted in America, and if they could convince me, then maybe I could convince my government to stop meddling in their affairs.

That all changed in the year 2000 when the second George Bush assumed the presidency of the United States, even though he received fewer overall votes than Al Gore. The election was decided in Florida, where thousands of votes from black precincts were discredited while George Bush's brother Jeb, the governor of Florida, picked the people who picked the people who picked the votes, based on a completely subjective process of determining which hanging chads of paper in the punched-out ballots would count.

If you lived in Chile under Pinochet, or Panama under Noriega, or Mexico under Lopez Portillo, or Cuba under Batista, then you know a fixed election when you see one. That's Ballot Tampering 101, and that it could happen on such a blatant scale in the grand old dame of democracy, it was like Superman wasn't super anymore.

Latinos just kind of lost faith. It got worse after the United States attacked Iraq in a war the world didn't want. For the first time in twenty-five years of traveling I was being judged not by my actions but by the actions of my government. If there was no hope in America, then there was no hope, and I held up my sunscreen-soaked hands.

"Don't blame me," I said. "I didn't vote for him either."

Chac stumbled sideways into a mangrove support post and caught himself on a forearm tapered like a bowling pin upholstered in hairless brown skin.

"The Corn Gods are coming to kick your ass," he said confidentially, "In . . . ," *Chac* stood, legs spread, and counted on his fingers until he reached the middle of his second hand, then said, "In eight years."

The ancient Mayans believed that life comes in cycles, and that this, the Fourth Creation, will end in the year 2012. It's close enough to the year 2000 end-of-the-world Christian prophecies to make you think twice.

"And your President knows it," continued *Chac*. "Because if he doesn't believe the world is ending, then why does he hand it such ugly treatment?"

What bothered me was that I'd read something uncannily similar in a newspaper I found on a seat at the Miami airport on the way down. The article was about rapture, the Christian bliss bestowed by God upon His return to earth to reward His chosen few. The gist of the article was that if you believed in rapture, and thought you were one of the Chosen few, then you probably couldn't wait for the world to end. If you believed in rapture, you might pollute the earth until even the air and oceans couldn't hold it all. That might be something you would do.

"I hate myself when I think that such an idea could be true," I said.

Chac grabbed up a bottle of *tequila*, poured a splash off in his mouth, then wiped his lips with the back of his hand.

"It is truth," he said. "In seven years your *gringo* ass is going down."

"Eight years," I said.

Chac's eyes glazed and he sank down onto a bench.

"Whatever," he said.

I didn't totally disagree with *Chac*. I spent most of my life in the outdoors and have never understood the headlong rush to pave this strange and wondrous planet. Life is too interconnected. Species are disappearing at a rate the planet hasn't seen in over two hundred million years. There's just too much evidence that when we wipe out other life forms we wipe out ourselves. Rapture might be a reason why a chosen few would pursue policies of planetary suicide, but I can tell you this.

I didn't want to believe it.

It was just too sad.

If anything, it seems to me, we should err on the side of being nice to Mother Nature, because Mother Nature can kick back. We should get back to phi. There's no telling what will happen as we approach the end of the Fourth Creation, but if it's anything like the end of the Third Creation, at least it won't be boring.

Back then, as the end of a whorl in the spiral of creation approached, corn was king. Corn gave the Mayan civilization life. Cultivated corn provided food for the cities to grow, and the Corn Gods were honored as youthful and exuberant deities who liked to while away the eons on the rectangular stone-walled ball court.

The goal in ball was to be first to toss a hardball of *chicle* through a sacred hoop. Violence was encouraged so it was a noisy game, and one day the Corn Gods were playing away when the ball court suddenly gave a great heave.

Voices came up through the ground. The Old Gods of the Underworld were annoyed.

"Hey you kids," said the Old Gods, "Keep it down up there. We're trying to sleep."

But boys will be boys, even when they're Gods.

"Fuddy-duddies," said the Corn Gods, and kept right on playing.

It was too much for the Underworld Lords, who built wooden statues of themselves, then sent owls to summon the boys. The Corn Gods whistled as they crossed the rivers of blood and corruption, then scoffed as they addressed the Underworld Lords.

"Is this the worst you can do?" laughed the Corn Gods.

But the Corn Gods had addressed the wooden statues, not the Underworld Lords. The Dark Lords came out from their hiding places, laughing at how they'd made the Corn Gods look foolish with their trick.

The name the French in the time of Marie Antoinette gave this form of political maneuvering was ridicule, and after laughing obnoxiously for too long the Lords of the Underworld offered the Corn Gods cigars and firewood to help pass the long night. The Corn Gods gladly accepted the hospitality, only to find out the next morning the Underworld Lords hadn't told them about the part where you had to give the wood and tobacco back untouched, on penalty of death.

"Not fair," said the Corn Gods.

"Is too," said the Underworld Lords.

The Underworld Lords held a trial and trumped up the charges. The Corn Gods were smeared with blue ointment, stretched, and sacrificed on the sacred rock. The bodies of the Corn Gods were buried under the ball court, but not before the Underworld Lords beheaded the older Corn God and propped his head in a thornbush as an example to noisy children everywhere.

Here's the thing. Corn is tough to kill. Cultivated corn is a powerful basis for a civilization, and the severed head of the Corn God was so fertile that he caused a thornbush to burst into glorious bloom. This then caused a beautiful Underworld Princess Babe to check out the flowers.

"Hey there," said Corn Head. "Come here often?"

"You're supposed to be dead," said Underworld Princess Babe.

"Our little secret," said Corn Head. "Would you mind moving this flower?"

Corn Head smiled a smile so brilliant you could almost overlook the fact that he came without a neck. Underworld Princess Babe reached out to move the flower that hung down in front of Corn Head's eye, and as she reached, Corn Head spit in her palm.

"Gotcha," said Corn Head, well pleased with His trick.

Just like that, Underworld Princess Babe was pregnant and had to leave town. If this account of an immaculate conception sounds familiar, it should. Mary got the same surprise with Jesus, but since Corn Head was so fertile Underworld Princess Babe gave birth to not one son but two.

She called them the Hero Twins, and her boys liked a good, rowdy game of ball just the same as their fathers. It was only a question of time until there was trouble.

"Who's making that racket this time?" whined the Old Gods of the Underworld.

The Hero Twins were summoned to another Underworld trial, and having been advised by their Mother what happened to their fathers the Corn Gods, the Twins enlisted the help of an animal helper: Mosquito.

Imagine: a religion that honors the mosquito. Human sacrifice aside, it gives you an idea of just how bloodthirsty the ancient Mayans really were.

At the tribunal, a gaunt Lord roared:

"How do you plead?"

"Not guilty," said the Hero Twins.

"Guilty," said the Underworld Lords, but this time their tricks didn't work.

The Hero Twins looked not at the gaunt Lord who was speaking, but at the holes in the rocks of the cave where the real Lords were hiding. Mosquito had gone ahead to nibble on the Lords and rat out the wooden imposters. Now it was the Twins who were laughing, even as they were imprisoned in the House of Knives, where they were charged with the overnight task of filling the House with flowers from a far-away garden.

The penalty for failure was death. There was no escape from a house built with walls of slashing knives, so the Hero Twins sent their friend Leaf-cutter Ant to bring the flowers they needed. One by one the Twins fulfilled a string of seemingly impossible tasks until finally the Underworld Lords gnashed their teeth in frustration and rage.

"How about a ball game?" proposed the Hero Twins. "Winner take all."

This was it. No more tricks. In the Mayan world, the buck stops at the ball court. It's put-up or shut-up time. The Hero Twins made mincemeat of the Underworld Lords, and as a reward for their play demanded the resurrection of their fathers, the Corn Gods.

Corn could again grow just as the Third Creation drew to a close when an Old World God, named "L," destroyed the world in a flood. He was such a bad dude; he didn't even have a name, just an initial, God L.

Have you ever heard of any other lusty vengeful Gods like that? A God who came down from heaven and made immaculate whoopee? A God who flooded his people out? A God who could manage a resurrection of the flesh?

The parallels between Mayan and Catholic belief are striking, and in the wake of the *conquistadors* the defeated Indians decided they lost because the Christians had stronger Gods. The Indians figured it wasn't their fault, it was their God's fault, and this sense of fatalism, the idea that you can't change what's already predetermined by the stars, has been passed through the generations until it's as much a part of Mexico as the *tortilla*.

When it comes to Gods, you want the best you can get, and Catholicism swept the New World. It was easy for the Mayans and Aztecs to accept this new Christian God because he was so much like their old Gods. Creationists believe Noah built his ark in 4004 B.C.; classic Mayans believe the Hero Twins emerged from the Underworld through a crack in the back of the cosmic turtle and arranged the hearth for the Fourth Creation in the shape of the triangle of stars surrounding the nebula in Orion's Belt on exactly August 13, 3114 B.C.

Five-hundred-and-forty-two days later (Mayan astronomers were very precise in their depiction of reality) the hearth was still curing as the Fourth Creation was completed with the erection of the four sides and corners of the Cosmos; and then, in the motion of weavers spinning thread, the Cosmos was sent to twirling about the North Star.

It was this spin that created time, gave order to the universe, and determined everything from the right day for your marriage to auspicious times to wage war on the next city-state down the jungle line. Ancient Mayans were extreme numerologists. The movements of the planets and stars didn't just speak, they commanded, that this, the Fourth Creation, would draw to a cataclysmic close.

In 2012.

Damn the environment, full speed ahead. Plundering is policy that makes perfect sense if the sky is falling and Rapture awaits. Maybe the world really is ending. Mayan Jaguar Priests were tuned into the planet in ways contemporary society isn't. It's possible they knew something we don't.

"Fucking *gringos*," said *Chac* as he closed his eyes.

Chac settled into a seat, laid his arm on the table, and put his head on his arm. I flopped around in my rubber flats booties helping *Pato* top off the red plastic gasoline tanks in the fiberglass boats locally known as *pangas. Chac* was snoring up little bubbles of spittle as the rest of the class arrived at the dock, and Mercury couldn't believe anybody could let themselves fall so low.

"Disgusting," he said. "Absolutely disgusting."

The truth is the five Mayan fishing guides on a bender didn't look all that different from a bunch of Wyoming cowboys lying around the morning after a big rodeo. At least nobody had thrown up on their girlfriend.

"Oh," I said, "I don't know."

The old guides lay sated amongst their beers, the twelve grinning novices determined to replace them climbed into the *pangas*, solid fiberglass boats built with high sides and a blunt heavy prow to beat down the waves. We roared away from the dock in two boats with the 65 horse Yamaha outboards held wide open.

The ride was dry, fast and smooth as the wake peeled off the notched transom into the blue-grey swell. Twenty-five knots into a fifteen knot headwind feels like a forty knot wind, a refreshing break from the humidity as we planed past a shoreline of low waxy green mangroves, but a poor time to carry on a conversation.

"Hey Mercury," I shouted, "Do you have . . ."

I lifted my chin from my chest just far enough for the wind to catch the brim of my hat and grabbed too late. *Pato* grinned as he put the *panga* on edge in a fast circle back.

"Wot?" yelled Mercury.

"It's nothing," I yelled back as I plucked my sopping hat from the water. "I'll tell you later."

I was going to ask Mercury if he had an idea for a lesson plan, but as we surged back up on plane, I got an idea. I could talk about the wind, which is a constant factor on the saltwater flats.

The wind can be your enemy, or it can be your friend. It all depends on your plan, and fifteen kilometers later *Pato* cut the throttle down to idle as we eased out of the wide blue bay and into a narrow green channel that opened into a three-lobed mangrove flat called *Paraíso*.

Paraíso means Paradise and it was exactly the kind of place I could spend eternity. This flat was alive. Coming in we spooked up a couple of barracuda, the big ones, four-footers. The bottom was everywhere pockmarked with the holes bonefish make when they feed, and off to the side a family unit of flamingoes worked a bar of limestone marl.

Ma and Pa Flamingo stood five feet tall and glowed electron pink. The whiter twin youngsters were half as tall and squabbling by beating each other with their wings as we dropped anchor in knee deep water. Behind the flamingoes, a centuries-old set of fitted stone steps led to the edge of the solid green jungle and stopped, which is more than I can say for the students as I stepped out of the boat into the tepid water to begin my spiel.

"*Hurakan*," I said.

Hurakan is the Mayan God of Wind. We know him today as a hurricane, which is what it looked like had hit the class as they blew off for the four corners of the cosmic turtle.

"Hey," I shouted. "Where's everybody going?"

Hurakan could fill your sails so you didn't have to paddle. He could also feed you to the Shark God or blow away your cities. The lesson was that you can't beat your Gods, you have to join them.

It's the same with guiding. You can fight the wind, or you can use it to your advantage.

"It all depends on your plan," I called out.

I was proud of my analogy and determined to use it, but calling for order was like trying to reign in momentum itself. Nobody graduated until they caught a fish, and twelve brown Mayans left twelve white wakes as they waded furiously in a race for the best spots on the flat.

"Hey," I shouted to their broad retreating backs. "Come back here!"

Deep down, I thought one of those prime fishing spots would be mine, and now every bonefish between here and *Cancun* had been spooked. Plus, I wanted the class to go out two students to one rod, to guide each other, to learn discipline, to practice their English.

We had a class to run here, Goddamn it.

I took a deep breath, filling up on air for the loudest scream I could muster when Mercury stepped in and drew his manicured fingernail like a knife across his throat.

"Let 'em go," he said. "For them it's like Christmas morning."

Going fishing with fly rods, some of them for the first time, it didn't get more exciting than that. The worst thing a guide can do is take the fun out of fishing. I'd been about to shout, to harangue, to impose an authority I did not have, and my lips flapped as I slowly let the air out of my lungs.

I'd been trying to fight the wind.

Over by the shore, Ma and Pa Flamingo splashed in on black knobby legs as long as broomsticks to separate their squawking children. I was acting like a petulant child myself, wallowing in self pity that I wouldn't get to go bonefishing. It took Mercury to set me straight; the sun gleamed off his bright bleached teeth as he smiled.

"It's like you been saying," he said. "You gawta have a plan. Let's go back after them barracuda."

Big barracuda are a blast on a fly rod. While I'd been pouting, Mercury had been thinking for the both of us.

"That's a great idea," I said.

"I'll pole," said Mercury.

Mercury said how he needed a good barracuda picture for his Web site as he poled us along in one of the *pangas*. I stood in the bow with a ten-weight rod rigged with a needlefish fly and wire tippet, and as we eased out toward the deeper water I had shots at four different barracuda.

The first two saw right through my little game. The fish ignored dozens of casts until finally they tired of the commotion and swam away. With the next barracuda I put the fly right on the fish's eye with the idea it might provoke an attack; the third barracuda just vaporized.

He left so quickly I never even saw him go. The fourth barracuda was silvery-blue and the largest yet, at least as long as my leg and nearly as thick. So far, the fish had ignored two casts I'd thrown about ten feet in front of his head.

I decided to change patterns and was stripping in the fly when a mutton snapper flashed up out of a coral head and hooked himself on my fly. A short tussle later I looked the olive-backed snapper right in his bright red eye.

"Sorry," I said. "It's in the interest of science."

The barracuda obviously knew we were there. What wasn't so obvious was whether the barracuda wouldn't eat because it knew we were there, or because it knew the flies were fakes. If the barracuda could resist a real live fish, it would imply that the barracuda had made the connection between humans and hooks. It would imply that barracuda are capable of deductive reasoning.

At least that's what I told Mercury. But we both knew what I was really doing was justifying bait-fishing for that big barracuda as I lobbed the mutton snapper in the right general direction.

The cast landed five yards short and to the left in the clear water. The barracuda flicked its forked tail once that I saw. The snapper dove for the bottom. The barracuda evaporated in one nanosecond and reappeared in the next, skipping through the waves like a blue torpedo at the end of my line.

The linked string of low flat jumps came so quickly that the whirring handle on my reel ripped a hunk of skin off my thumb before I could think to move my hand. The blood hadn't even begun to drip yet and the barracuda was fifty meters into my backing.

Barracuda are built for speed not endurance. The first run is the best, at the end of the fight it's like pulling in a log. The barracuda stretched twice the width of my shoulders. The once blue back was now grey with lactic fatigue as I held the barracuda up, but I didn't care how tired it was. I was still a little nervous holding up a fish with a mouth that was ten inches long and full of sharp pointed teeth.

"Get it quick," I said.

Mercury snapped a picture, then looked behind me and waved as I slid the fish overboard.

"Here dey come," he said.

One by one the Mayans were returning to where we'd left the other *panga* anchored. We poled over, and *Pancho*, the most experienced fly fisherman of the lot, held up four fingers.

"*Cuatro*," he said.

The next three Mayans hadn't been so lucky.

"*Nada*," they all said, "Nothing."

Out of the bunch, *Pancho* took honors with four fish. Nobody else had more than two. Half the students hadn't even had hookups. Twelve Mayans had landed a total of eleven fish. We had a lot to learn and not long to learn it in. When the entire class was reassembled I said that what struck me was that Mayans had been fishing this very same flat for five thousand years.

"And it's a good thing they had nets," I said, "Because with flies they might have starved to death."

The Mayans who caught fish laughed appreciatively. The Mayans who hadn't, frowned.

"And because of this," I said, "Nobody graduation without everybody graduation."

One by one smiles became frowns and frowns became smiles as the students deciphered my Spanish. Nobody graduated unless everybody graduated, and if nobody graduated unless they caught a fish, that meant nobody graduated unless everybody caught a fish.

"Here is the thing," I said. "No more running like that. It's a terrible thing for a guide to do. Wait for the client. It signifies nothing if you see the fish and the client is not prepared to cast. The only thing that is lost is an opportunity."

"And your tip," said Mercury.

"Always, always, always," I said, "Wait for the client."

The loudest sound was the waves lapping at the hull of the boats as I paused.

"Tomorrow," I said, "For two students, only one rod. One person is the guide, one is the client. Practice fishing, but practice guiding. Have a plan. Give a service. Teach."

The class ranged in fly-fishing experience from none to some. My hope in staking the success of the individual to the success of the group was that the students who could already catch fish would teach those who couldn't. The more experienced students would learn guiding, the less experienced students would learn fishing, and we'd all learn language.

We'd be teaching to the highest common denominator, not the lowest, and the plan worked, mostly. In many ways *Pato* was the best guide there, but four days later, on the last afternoon of the last class, he still hadn't landed a fish.

And nobody graduated until he did.

I'd said it out loud. I had to live up to it. But what if nobody graduated? That wouldn't be right either. Everybody had worked so hard. But if I doubted, Mercury never did.

"See you tonight," he said. "It may be late."

For our last afternoon together as a class we were back at *Paraíso* sharing the flat with dozens and dozens of hard-feeding flamingos. Mercury sloshed off with *Pato* into the green mangrove lee of the right lobe of the three-fingered flat. Mercury, as they walked, held out one arm and pulled back with the other, demonstrating a strip-strike, his voice booming as they disappeared around the corner.

"Strip strike," he said. "You gawta strip strike."

"Streep strike," repeated *Pato*. "Streep strike."

As for me, this was my time. The class had been an utterly fulfilling experience. It had also been a lot of work, and since I wasn't getting paid in money, I figured I might as well get paid in flamingos, and I angled off for the main flock.

At least fifty birds formed a ragged line, shockingly pink and five feet tall, with long necks like scarlet snakes trailing heads that stayed beak down to the water for minutes at a time. The flamingos were feeding hard from right to left on a shallow turtle-grass shelf, and as I snapped a few pictures, a school of tailing bonefish slid in on the falling tide.

The bonefish poked up their silver tails and dorsal fins, wallowing in the shin deep water as they fed in the midst of the thicket of stout flamingo legs. Birds and fish, grazing along together like they were part of the same herd, completely absorbed in feeding, they had to be eating the same food.

Flamingos are pink because of the carotene in the shrimp they eat; therefore, it seemed almost certain that the correct fly to use to catch those fish would be a pink shrimp.

It seemed like a no-brainer, and I started with a bright pink shrimp with trailing black eyes. When that didn't work I went to a dull pink shrimp, then a little pink shrimp, then a big pink shrimp. Then brown, green, and blue shrimp. Then some crabs; big, little, shiny and dull. Then more pink shrimp, a couple of baitfish patterns, a sea urchin and finally a weird flat fly tied to look like a clam.

With increasing desperation, I tried fly after fly. It wasn't like I didn't get shots. I bet I cast twenty different patterns to fifty different fish without so much as a follow. I'd bounce the fly off their exposed backs and the bonefish didn't even have the decency to spook. They'd just scoot over a couple of feet and resume gorging.

Birds and fish, they gave me all the respect they would a clump of mangrove. The clucking flamingos were so close I could smell the heat baking in their ripe wet feathers, at the bird's feet bonefish were half-out of the water and wriggling like silver snakes.

In the Mayan world everything was alive, and nothing was as it seemed. The sky was a serpent, directions were colors. The curved earth was the shell on the back of a slowly crawling turtle. Reality had layers, alternate universes that coexisted in the same space-time fabric, which meant that there were two sides to everything.

Consider a tree from the Mayan point of view.

Is a tree of the air, or of the ground? Is a tree of the rain, or the dirt? A worm living its whole life in the roots would think it knew the tree, but would know nothing of the leaves. A bird living in the leaves would think it knew the tree, yet would know nothing of the wood that would eventually form a canoe. Layer upon layer, that's how the Mayans saw their world. You couldn't trust your eyes, not if you expected to see anything.

The ancient Mayans visualized this, the Fourth Creation, as a giant *Ceiba* tree rooted on the southern horizon. The otherwise limbless and smooth-barked tree has a curling top-knot of branches that supports the Milky Way, but trees die. The stars will come crashing down. It's fate and it's coming no matter how many realities you cling to.

The dual nature of my own reality was that on the most beautiful evening of my life I was fated to get skunked. Whatever those fish were eating, I couldn't figure it out. The reflection of the slowly sinking sun stained the water first yellow then orange then oily red, until finally there was no choice but to wade back to the *pangas* for the boat ride home.

That a setting sun would rise the following morning was not something the Mayans took for granted. At dusk the life-giving Sun metamorphosed into the mighty Jaguar God, who all night long had to fight His way from the west through the nine levels of Underworld hell to the safety of the eastern ocean, where the Sun could be born anew each dawn.

It was a tough journey so the Jaguar Priests helped the sun along with ritual transfusions of blood. When it comes to the Mayans and blood, think war. The powerful city-states during the classic period fought huge battle after huge battle against a political backdrop of betrayal and intrigue.

Political alliances shifted constantly as the various kings switched allegiances as the stars commanded. The enemy of your enemy was your friend. Over the centuries a slew of kings died of poison or stab wounds, compliments of cousins plotting to ascend to the throne themselves.

In the midst of the destruction, merchants prayed to God "L," the really bad dude who flooded the world at the end of the Third Creation. No king in his right mind would mess with God L, because he protected the merchant class.

Roads were built and trade flourished. Commodities as varied as magic mushrooms, sea salt, cacao beans, rubber and jade were traded over distances of hundreds of miles. Discerning Jaguar Priests throughout the jungle empire prized the spines of stingrays, which they used to pierce the penis; the blood was then dripped on sacred paper and burned as an offering to the Gods.

Mayans ruled Central America for nearly a thousand years, but if there's any doubt why they abandoned their cities around A.D. 900 just read that last sentence again. The noble elite were getting into some kinky shit. Ritual sacrifice had begun with iguanas and turkeys, but the soft stuff led to the hard stuff, until finally only human blood would do.

The Jaguar Priests sliced their way up through captive slaves to princesses and finally stonewashed, homegrown virgin peasant girls. Imagine the power those priests wielded, knowing, to the moment, when a solar eclipse was due.

They could have picked the day to pack a hundred-thousand sweating Mayan peasants into the ceremonial plazas beneath the altars in the stone temples. It would be pinned to the second, the jungle drums beating faster and faster, louder and louder, whipping the mob to a frenzy, and at the exact instant the last starlight-filtered twinkle disappears and the earth is plunged into darkness the jade knife plunges and a death-scream rings out as blood spurts on the stone altar.

Now that's giving the crowd what they want. That's better than the Super Bowl and Roman gladiators all rolled into one. I felt almost enlightened by what I'd learned from the Mayans over the course of the class, but the mood was subdued as we gathered back at the *pangas*.

Nobody had done very well. Nobody had figured it out, and everybody was anxious about Mercury and *Pato*. Would there be a graduation or not? It was out of my hands as I sat on a *panga* sucking a beer, marveling at the view as the various Lords of Day and Night traded places in the ocean land Where the Sky is Born again each Mayan day.

Venus was blue-bright in the sky as Mercury and *Pato* appeared in the dusk, trailing turbulent wakes in the mirror of the sunset-stained water. The two of them walked stride for stride the way they always walked, like they were going to live forever.

I knew, right off the bat, from Mercury's sly grin.

"How did you do it?" I asked.

Mercury held up a fly they'd trimmed down with scissors until it was nothing but a tiny bit of bright pink fur on a mostly bare hook.

"*Pato* figured it out," he said. "It was because of what he knew flamingos eat."

For the record, I checked later. Flamingos do eat shrimp, but the giant birds eat the smallest of prey. Flamingos are filter feeders, straining microorganisms through special plates in their heavy black bills. The shrimp they eat are measured on the order of microns.

Even the smallest flies in my box were too big by a factor of ten. Wiggling brine shrimp on No. 80 hooks, that's what the bonefish were eating. No matter what you know, you can always learn more. That's something that fly-fishing can teach you about life, and the rest of us all looked around at each other as we figured it out.

There was going to be a graduation. Not only that, as a class we now knew how to catch those fish that had so dogged us. At least someone had dialed into it, and jubilation reigned.

"*¿Quántos? ¿Quántos?*" said everybody at once.

It means "How many?" and Mercury held up three fingers on each hand.

"Seex," he said.

Mercury then put a proud right arm around *Pato's* shoulder. The rich New Yorker, the poor Mayan, I'll tell you, it was enough to bring a tear to my eye.

"Tell 'em," said Mercury. "How'd we do?"

Pato showed the gold caps on his two front teeth in a smile that spanned cultures and, if his ancestors had it right, universes. Brown and squat, *Pato* gleamed like the Jaguar God in the fading light, but he sounded more like a taxi driver in the Bronx as he said:

"We moiduh'ed duh bums."

THE MORE THINGS CHANGE . . .
THE MORE THEY STAY THE SAME

These days we meet for coffee with nondairy creamer but in the good old days we met for high-fat beers. Back then, a fishing trip could happen at any moment, even the middle of the night, and the point of germination was often a neighborhood saloon called Big Dorothy's.

Big Dorothy's is tucked up against the pine covered Montana mountains, and if the granite walls in what is now a friendly south side tavern could tell their story they wouldn't just talk. The walls would also scream and moan because Big Dorothy was the proprietress of what in its day had been regarded as one of the great western whorehouses.

Big Dorothy is gone now, but the historic building remains. I was sitting on a stool at the original bar one night, happily engaged in a baseless fantasy that beautiful Becky the brown-eyed bartender might one day sleep with me, when the swinging front doors burst open. It was the tall wide Duke and the short wide Mayor, striding along in a synchronized goose step that said something was in the wind.

"Hey, boys," said Becky.

"What's up?" I asked.

Duke and the Mayor bulled in close on either side.

"The Bugs," said the Duke.

He picked up the fresh draft beer in front of me, drank half of it off in great thirsty gulps, and then extended the thick glass mug handle-first to the Mayor. The Mayor finished the beer off and sighed with satisfaction.

"They're coming," he said.

The Bugs are Salmon Flies, lumbering orange stone-flies the size of a woman's thumb, and enough of a meal to make even big fish stupid. A big smile hung in the bottom of the Duke's oval face as he raised three fingers.

"Wild Turkey for my friends," he said.

For a while there not all American women shaved their underarms and Becky in her spaghetti-strap top flashed a dainty pocket of fine dark hair as she reached for a bottle on the top shelf.

"Bugs," she said. "What is it you guys see in all these bugs anyway?"

"Magic," I said.

"Adventure," said the Duke.

"A reason to miss work," said the Mayor.

If you're a fly-fisherman, a thick hatch of Salmon Flies is a natural wonder not to be missed. They look prehistoric because they are prehistoric. The stone fly family is among the oldest of the living insects, and dates back to the Carboniferous Age 340-million-years-ago.

The Carboniferous was a boisterous time on planet Earth because life was making the first dedicated break for higher ground. At that point, the land was pretty much just rocks and dirt. There were land plants around, including giant ferns, but these plants were dependent for reproduction on spores that germinated only if they fell directly in the water.

Plants had made it away from the Mother Ocean only as far as the swamps, and it was same with animals. Amphibians and tetrapods were breathing air and crawling around in the mud, but their eggs had to be laid in water and remain in water in order to be fertilized and hatch.

Reptiles answered the siren call of the wide open spaces of empty habitat with the development of the amniotic egg which didn't desiccate on dry ground. Plants developed seeds which could dry out without dying and marched up the hills. Insects left the water behind with the most stunning adaptation of all: they learned to fly.

To me, that's magic.

How they did it, nobody knows.

Somehow, all those eons ago, while crawling around in the rocks and mud of those ancient swamp bottoms, swimming insects with gills figured out how to grow wings and fly. It's called metamorphosis, an evolutionary advantage so complete it hasn't changed much to this day.

Salmon fly hatches are notoriously fickle. The Bugs are here today and gone tomorrow. If you wait, you might miss it, but there wasn't much chance of that.

"When are we leaving?" I asked.

The Duke wiped beer foam off his upper lip with the back of his hand, then wiped his hand on his pants.

"Early," he said.

"Real early," added the Mayor.

Becky looked at me like I was a science project.

"Don't you even care where you're going?" she said.

Only because I wondered how long we'd be gone.

"Where are we going?" I asked.

Duke and the Mayor couldn't quit smiling.

"The Smith," said the Duke.

The Smith River is sixty-five miles of wild limestone canyon. Access is limited. The only way out is to float and it's usually a five day trip. If you got hurt, you stayed hurt, and I looked at the clock on the wall.

"What day is it?" I asked.

"Last time I checked," said the Mayor, "Monday."

That meant I wouldn't have to sit at my desk job for the whole rest of the week. Answering machines had just been invented, a boon when you're calling in sick to work from a bar at midnight. I dropped a dime in the pay phone on the wall, lied for a while, and then came back to my stool.

"What did you tell them this time?" said the Duke.

"That I broke my finger," I said.

The Mayor narrowed his big grey eyes.

"Isn't that what you told them last time?" he said.

"No," I said, "That was my toe."

Becky pulled three iced mugs from the freezer and poured three draft beers.

"A broken toe," she said, "I can see faking that. You could just walk around the office with a limp for a while. But what are you going to do when you get back to work and your finger isn't broken?"

"He heals fast," said the Duke.

The Mayor is organized and likes lists. He grabbed a pen from behind the bar, started writing out what we didn't want to forget on a cocktail napkin, and then turned to me.

"Can you drive?" he asked.

Back then, I drove. I always drove. I had the pick-up truck, a bright orange Dodge named Julius I bought at a Highway Department auction for seven hundred dollars.

"I'll drive," I said.

Julius was pretty much always geared up for a week of fishing. I liked driving because it meant I was already packed, I didn't like driving because sometimes Julius broke down.

"We'll take my raft," said the Mayor.

I had Julius but the Mayor had the banana boat, a four-teen-foot canary-yellow raft with a wooden rowing frame and high-floating twenty-inch tubes.

"I'll get the food," said the Duke.

The Mayor and I spoke as one voice.

"No way."

The last time Duke got food he brought four dozen doughnuts and three gallons of Bloody Mary mix. That wouldn't have been so bad, except that's all he'd brought.

"I'll bring the meat," said the Mayor.

The Mayor is a hard-core carnivore and has a freezer full of prime elk, deer, and antelope. When you get used to wild meat, cow just isn't the same.

"For everything else," I said, "Let's just hit a grocery store on the way out of town."

"Everything else," said the Duke, "Except the gin."

Becky leaned in on her side of the bar and smiled.

"I can sell you some gin," she said.

The Duke leaned in on his side of the bar and smiled.

"Give me the good stuff," he said.

The Mayor put down the pen and scratched his head.

"Can I borrow your lipstick?" he said.

"He must be talking to you," I told Becky.

Becky gave the Mayor a tube of gloss lipstick; he used it to make big bright red "X" on the back of his hand.

"You gonna mail yourself back to your mother?" said Becky. "Because if you are, maybe you ought to warn her you're coming."

A bald spot gleamed as the Mayor shook his head.

"No," he said. "That's so I don't forget to put the ante-lope on the manifold."

The Mayor is an ordained master of manifold cookery, the technique of roasting meals on the engine as you drive. With our next meal taken care of there was only one thing left to decide.

"Well," I said. "We could either sleep for a couple of hours . . . or we could just stay up."

"It ain't that near closing time," observed Becky.

In the old days we made it look easy. It was still dark as I drove Julius across the street from the grocery store to the gas station on the way out of town. A pimply faced kid on a ladder was changing the plastic numbers that gave the price of leaded gasoline on the sign out front.

"Hate to see that," said the Mayor.

Gas, for the first time, was up to a dollar a gallon and with trouble in the mid-east there was no end in sight to the price hikes. I filled up the tank, the Duke washed the windows, and the Mayor lifted the orange hood of the truck and placed a duct-tape and aluminum-foil wrapped package on the manifold between the carburetor and the alternator.

Orion gleamed in a moonless sky as I steered Julius away from the gas pump and onto the two-lane highway. The Mayor sat in the middle on the front bench seat reading the sports page of a newspaper by the light of a headlamp; against the far door the Duke leaned forward playing air guitar along with Z. Z. Topp on the stereo as the headlights cut the night.

"So," I said, "Is there going to be an Olympics?"

The Mayor pulled his nose up out of the paper.

"It doesn't look good," he said. "A bunch of other coun-tries are pulling out."

The Soviet Union had invaded Afghanistan over the winter, and in protest, the United States was organizing a boycott of the summer Olympics which were being held that year in Moscow. I was a competitive swimmer all my life and couldn't imagine what it would be like to be good enough to go to the Olympics and then not get to go.

"I don't know about this boycott," I said. "It's hard to see how it's going to help stop a war."

"In the last four-thousand years nobody's ever invaded Afghanistan successfully," said the Mayor. "You wait and see. Time will take care of the Russians."

The Mayor stuck his nose back into the box scores and I kept Julius between the lines. It's a hundred-and-fifty-three miles over the mountains from Big Dorothy's to the un-mowed field where you launch your boat into the Smith River. The sun was up, but below the limestone canyon walls, as I turned off the engine and we stepped out onto cold frosted bunchgrass that crunched beneath our river sandals.

"Anybody hungry?" said the Mayor.

We'd stopped to flip the package on the manifold once, and for the whole last hour the taste of the antelope roast as it bubbled away in its own juices had been wafting into the cab through the defrost vents.

"I'm starving," I said.

The Mayor slit the triple-wrapped layer of foil and duct tape, pulled it back like a bowl, then cut a half-pound chunk off the end of the roast with a bone-handled skinning knife.

"Meat," he said. "It isn't just for breakfast anymore."

The Mayor comes by his carnivorous instincts honestly. Eating meat is a development that seemingly characterizes us as people. Two-and-a-half million years ago the human genus *Homo* was distinguished by a sudden increase in brain size, simultaneously with the use of stone tools and the addition of meat to the diet.

Meat contains several different proteins, and these proteins are the building blocks of the neurotransmitters that allow us to think. It makes sense that with more protein you could have more thoughts, a cranial development that led directly from stone spears to the creation of the stock market, reality television, and Spam.

Meat isn't just mammals. It's also fish. Among the tools discovered by archaeologists in those earliest of human camps are fish hooks. In my experience humans who fish are generally happy humans, possibly because people have been fishing ever since they've been people.

Fish really is brain food. It's possible fishing scratches core atavistic itches we don't even know we have. It could be that fishing reduces stress by working on the ninety-nine percent of the brain that is subconscious, or in my case, unconscious.

"Has anybody seen my socks?" I asked.

The Duke looked up from the two-burner green Coleman stove where he was making coffee.

"No," he said, "But I have an extra pair of mittens."

I knew I'd seen my thick wool socks around, but they weren't with my waders like they usually were. My feet were cold in the frosted bunchgrass, and the Mayor looked at me like no matter what else happened in life, at least he didn't have to be me.

"Your socks are on the air filter," he said. "Right where you left them."

Now I remembered. I was warming them up, an idea I'd stolen from the art of manifold cookery.

"Eureka," I said.

The socks had warmed up nicely on the flat metal housing to the engine's air filter, and made the job of pulling on frozen neoprene waders much more comfortable. My toes weren't even numb as we chewed meat, drank coffee, and unpacked the truck.

Before too long we had the banana boat inflated, loaded, in the river, and tied off to a wooden fence post. Duke and the Mayor rigged to flip by lashing down gear while I locked up Orange Julius, and then walked the short hill to the shuttle tree, where I left a spare key and twenty bucks in the rusty tin can under the flat rock for the shuttle driver.

Back at the river the Duke was standing in the water at the stern of the banana boat; the Mayor was sitting at the oars with a doughnut in one hand and a doughnut in the other.

"I wonder what the poor people are doing today," he said.

The Duke took a drag on his cigarette then waved his arm at the big white cooler that was the seat in the open bow.

"Your throne," he said, "Awaits."

When fly-fishing from a moving boat, the bow is far and away the best place to be. Especially in the banana boat, because the guy in the back didn't have so much a seat as a perch atop a mound of camping gear. If you weren't careful, you could fall in. I didn't mind starting out in the front.

"Cool," I said.

The Mayor looked at his watch and smiled at our efficiency. In terms of pulling a trip together from scratch it had been one of our best efforts ever.

"Eight A.M." he said.

The Duke pushed us off from shore.

"Time to go to work," he said.

I toasted with my insulated coffee cup.

"I'll drink to that," I said.

Once you commit yourself to the current of a river there's no going back. Few acts in life feel as free as pushing off from land and giving yourself over to the water, and the

Smith is a lively and turbulent free-stone stream that plots a weaving course through the rock gardens that tumble from the towering ramparts of grey Madison Limestone.

The Madison is old limestone, as old as stone flies, and also dates back to the Carboniferous. At the time, Montana was covered by a shallow inland sea.

In the deeper water, calcium rich shellfish piled up into homogenous ooze thousands of feet thick that eventually became the Madison Limestone. In the shallow water swamps at the edge of higher ground, life was anything but homogenous. Seed-bearing plants reaching for the open land had worked a wonder of organic chemistry.

Early plants, growing toward the sun, relied for support on an ample supply of water to swell their cells. A little cell-shriveling drought, the plants would go limp and fall over. Clearly, there had to be a better way.

Plants, from toxic algae to chili peppers, have always had the knack of creating organic chemicals. Carboniferous plants solved the problem of rigidity by removing water from sugar in such a way the water couldn't return, thus manufacturing an organic hydrocarbon called lignin.

Lignin is what gives wood strength. It's tough stuff, that lignin. Even today it can take centuries to rot a cypress tree. Back then lignin was so strange and new that existing planetary life couldn't digest it. The lignin didn't decompose. It just piled up into thick organic mats, the hydrocarbon reserves that were eventually squeezed into the coal and oil that fueled the industrial revolution of man some 300-million-years-later.

Lignin is another of those developments upon which nature never really improved. It's still how trees grow tall, and the grey cliffs of Smith River limestone are pocked with green pine and fir. Tiny niches and ledges on the sheerest of faces are prime building sites for all manner of birds of prey, and the shrill piercing cry of a red-tailed hawk echoed down the canyon as we floated away from shore.

Behind me, on top of the gear mound, the Duke pulled a plastic box of flies from his grass-stained vest.

"What are you using?" I said.

He held up a two-inch-long black-hackled fly with a flowing black marabou tail and a green chenille body.

"I'm gonna bugger 'em up," he said.

In 1980 the Woolly Bugger was a new fly on the scene, and it caught so many fish, it was hard not to use it. Besides, the Duke caught more fish than anybody. If he thought it was a good idea, it probably was.

When it came to fishing anyway.

You could take the Duke's advice about fishing, but you had to be leery when it came to his suggestions about everything else. The Duke could just plain tolerate more stimulation than most of God's creatures except for maybe a bull elephant.

"Sounds good to me," I said.

A dark brown or black Woolly Bugger, with maybe a little bit of orange in it, drifted along the banks and ledges, would imitate the salmon fly nymphs crawling from the river to the shore during the hatch. Even with six legs some nymphs lose their footing on the slippery rocks and tumble away in the currents. Winter-hungry trout will key on these big squirming bugs, and the Duke fired a cast toward the bubbling shelf where Sheep Creek pours in from river right.

"Got one," he said.

A foot long brown trout jumped two feet in the air.

"Good on you," said the Mayor.

I cast to the other side of the boat, in a pocket along the willow bank, felt the smack and pulled back, too late.

"Missed him," I said.

"Nice one, farmer," said the Mayor.

A farmer obviously isn't a fisherman but I didn't farm for long. I picked up the line and tossed the fly back in the same pocket. This time I was ready, and now two brown trout jumped, one on each side of the boat.

"Hold on boys," said the Mayor. "We're going in."

The Smith is not a big river, especially at the upper end. It was either run the banana boat aground or take the narrow channel that scraped the left bank, which meant we plowed right over the top of my fish. The Mayor pulled hard right on the oars, and my fish, snubbed up on a short line, beat at the thin bottom of the raft against my feet.

Sometimes catching fish right off the bat like that is the kiss of death and you never get another one all day. This was not to be one of those days. The action was furious, and only a couple of bends into the canyon I'd already lost count of fish to the boat.

"How many is that?" I asked.

"Six," said the Mayor.

"Nine," said the Duke.

"I bet we could get a hundred today," said the Mayor.

"Maybe if anybody could count that high," I said.

The problem with counting is that you lose track. The Mayor let go of an oar for a second so he could finish his last doughnut before he proposed a solution.

"How about if we name these fish?" he said. "In alphabetical order. Like hurricanes. That way we could remember."

"Sure," said the Duke, "Three times through the alphabet, that's a hundred fish."

"Four times," I said.

"Do I hear five?" said the Mayor.

You can see the problem.

"How are we going to keep track of how many times we've been through the alphabet?" I asked.

"We need categories," said the Mayor. "One for each alphabet."

"What do you want to start with?" I asked.

Duke was catching a fish and the Mayor was rowing away from a rock but their minds were in the same place.

"Girls," they said.

You have to catch a fish every five minutes for over eight straight hours to get a hundred. I'd always wondered if it could even be done, but if ever there was a day to do it, we were in the right place at the right time.

Salmon fly nymphs are two inches long and eat other bugs. Salmon fly nymphs are carnivorous. They bite back, so the trout weren't just mouthing our flies, they were crushing them in smashing attacks meant to kill on the first chomp.

Figuring six trout so far, we started our first alphabet at Gina and ran it through Penny before the Mayor at the oars had finally had enough and pulled for the shore.

"It's time for somebody else to row," he said. "You guys are having way too much fun."

The Duke looked down at his waders.

"I have to get rid of some coffee anyway," he said.

The Mayor backed the boat toward a gravel bar on an inside bend, I threw one last cast toward a foam pocket in the dangling roots of an undercut bank. The foam bulged, and an eighteen inch trout leapt yellow-bellied against a backdrop of dried wheatgrass in the morning sunshine.

"Q," I said. "Now that's a tough one."

"Queenie," said the Duke. "I knew a Queenie once."

"I'll just bet you did," said the Mayor.

Most names came with a story, and after we'd heard that one, the Mayor scratched at his green wool shirt.

"Do you think girls talk about us?" he asked. "You know, the way we talk about them?"

"They're worse," I said.

Men talk about who they'd like to do it to and why, but women talk about how they did it. When it comes to pillow talk, most women are way raunchier than most men.

"It's why those romance novels sell so well," I said. "You ever read one of those things? They're filthy."

"My Grandma had a whole stack of those romances," said the Duke. "She kept them covered up with a towel in her clothes closet."

The Mayor looked worried as we ground ashore.

"What were you doing in your grandmother's closet?" he said.

"Playing hide and seek," said the Duke.

We got out and pulled the banana boat up onto the rocks so it wouldn't float away without us, then spread out along the bushes to pee. My stiff back cracked in three places as I stretched, then once more as I twisted.

In the shade of the cliff the morning was still cool enough that our breath condensed in hard white spurts. Ten steps out of the shadow and into the sun it was getting hot as we gathered back at the boat. The Duke was already settled in and champing at the oars.

"I'll row," he said.

A raft is like life because you can't stay up front forever. There's always somebody ready to take your place.

"I'll take the back," I said.

The Mayor and I dragged the banana boat out into the deeper water. He climbed into the bow and sat on the cooler, and I climbed up the flattopped pyramid of gear in the stern and sat on what felt like a couple cases of beer. I was still looking around for a life preserver to use as a cushion for my bony butt when the Mayor had his first fish.

"Rita," he said.

"Wasn't she the bear biologist?" said the Duke.

The Mayor smiled remembering the bare biologist when we'd all gone skinny-dipping in the cool Dearborn River on the way back from the sweaty Augusta Rodeo.

"She sure was," he said.

The sun, finally showing itself in the blue sky at the top of the grey canyon walls, was toasting the day up nicely. We'd all shed a layer of clothing by the time we ran the alphabet from Susan to Zoe and needed a new category.

"How about baseball?" said the Mayor.

The Duke held his hand flat and wiggled it.

"N-n-n-u-h-h," he said.

The Mayor loves baseball—like religion—from the first pitch on opening day, but the Duke could care less about sports. It's funny because the Duke goes two-fifty and used to play some ball. I guess it just goes to show that too much of anything and you can grow to hate what you once loved.

"How about politics?" I said.

I'm liberal and the Duke hugs trees, but the Mayor is extreme. From the lessons of Watergate and Vietnam to the environmental truths of Earth Day, our generation was going to make a difference. What we were against was the establishment, and the category became words to describe the power-brokers of industry and politics we so loved to hate.

"Assholes."

"Bastards."

"Cretins."

"I can't wait until we get to douche bag,"

The list went on as we floated, interspersed with fine liberal commentary on the current events of the day.

"Operation Eagle Claw," said the Duke. "Where do they come up with these names?"

"It's an insult to eagles everywhere," I said.

"Operation Eagle Shit," said the Mayor. "That's more like it."

Operation Eagle Claw was a recent American military maneuver in Iran, where for the thirty previous years British and American oil interests in collaboration with their respective governments had been propping up the totalitarian regime of the Shah. This hit at the core of the establishment's greedy underbelly. Everything needed to change.

The Shah of Iran was a cruel, brutal and murderous thug of a dictator, even by Middle Eastern-standards, who, in exchange for a lavish lifestyle and a secret police force to call his own, allowed big oil to siphon off the profits. In the midst of all that wealth the people of Iran should have at least been provided health insurance; what they got instead were death squads. This went on for decades, until finally a fundamentalist Muslim cleric named Ayatollah Khomeini inspired the people of Iran to revolt.

The rebellion was successful and the Shah was overthrown. Political maneuvering began immediately to reinstall the Shah on the puppet throne, and as a hole card against further foreign meddling, the Iranian rebels seized over a hundred United States citizens and held them hostage.

"Promise not to interfere in Iranian internal politics," said the Ayatollah, "And I'll let the hostages go."

Arabs barter. It's how they do business, and the hostages were useful as bargaining chips only as long as they were alive. The Ayatollah didn't want to kill the hostages. He wanted to let them go, but he wanted something in return.

He wanted to be left alone.

"No way," replied Uncle Sam.

Jimmy Carter was President. It was an election year, he was dropping in the polls, and he couldn't do a deal because it would make him appear weak. The country wouldn't stand for it. Besides, Carter had given away the Panama Canal and lots of people hated him for it. Carter was vilified in the conservative press as a spineless peanut farmer, when in fact he kept us out of a war with Iran we could not win.

Carter had to do something proactive, so he told the Army to work it out with the Marines and the Air Force. He told the combined forces to go in there and get those hostages. He told them to go do their job. He told them to stage a rescue.

On the ground, Operation Eagle Claw quickly turned to shit. Out of nine original rescue helicopters two broke down, one crashed on landing, and that was just trying to set up a base camp in the desert. The rescue mission was aborted in the midst of a raging sandstorm, and when the soldiers attempted to retreat, a fourth helicopter clipped a transport plane killing eight and wounding four.

As you might expect, everybody blamed everybody else. It wasn't anybody's fault, because it was everybody's fault, that's what was coming out daily in the papers.

The hostage rescue mission had been botched so badly because of a turf war amongst the pertinent American military agencies. It's like they were trying to fail. Nobody told each other the whole truth and nothing but the truth. Army, Marines, Air Force, C.I.A.; everybody was trying to take the credit, so everybody was holding something back.

Interagency secrecy happens because whoever gets the credit gets to ask Congress for more money at budget time, and it's the same failure to communicate that led to the destruction of the World Trade Center. In a quarter century, the people in charge, it's like they haven't learned a thing.

"Morons," said the Mayor.

He'd hooked a rainbow just as I was releasing a brown.

"Nincompoops," I said.

If you have a big stick, and you wave it, and it doesn't work, then your stick isn't so big anymore. The attempt to rescue the hostages in Iran couldn't have gone more poorly, and out of the whole mess, one thing bothered me most.

"You know what I can't understand?" I said.

The Mayor shook his fish off the hook.

"What happens to your tax dollars?" he said.

"That too," I said. "What I can't understand is, with all those surveillance satellites they're putting in the sky, how they missed a sandstorm the size of Vermont."

"It's like nobody ever told them that there are storms in the desert," said the Mayor.

"They should have watched more French Foreign Legion movies," said the Duke.

"You'd think they would have at least thought to put screens over the intakes to keep the sand out of the helicopter engines," I said.

"You'd think," said the Mayor.

"Did you see the new polls?" said the Duke. "Carter is way down."

"It isn't Carter's fault the helicopters crashed," I said.

The Duke feathered the long wooden oars with his ham-sized paws, backing us off so the Mayor and I could cast our flies tight to the deep bend where the river pushed against a sheer stone cliff covered with orange lichens.

"I still think this botched rescue is going to cost Carter the election," said the Duke.

The Mayor snorted at the impossibility of it all.

"Who's going to beat him?" he said. "Ronald Reagan?"

"Reagan beat Bush," said the Duke, "And nobody thought that was possible."

At the time, in the middle of May, Ronald Reagan was only a few votes away from securing the Republican nomination for the 1980 Presidential election. He'd beat out the pre-primary favorite George Bush, who was a few years off a stint as head of the CIA.

"Orangutan," I said.

"Orangutan?" said the Duke.

"It was the best I could come up with," I said.

The hook-jawed brown at the end of my line belly flopped against the backdrop of the limestone wall as the Mayor yanked back on his rod to jab the hook home. My trout went left, his torpedoed twice to the right, crossing our lines.

"Philanderer," said the Mayor.

"Good one," I replied.

The Mayor and I switched rods to uncross the lines and played the double around the bend. The trout came to the banana boat together, fat and golden-bellied with big red spots, eighteen-inch clones like we'd been catching one after another as we floated deeper and deeper into the canyon.

"Here's the thing," said the Duke, "Television changes the entire election process. If you aren't good on TV, you can't get elected any more."

With a string of mostly B-westerns to his credit Ronald Reagan hadn't exactly risen to the top of his craft, but he was a better actor than anybody else on the political stage.

"And television takes money," continued the Duke, "So whoever raises the most money wins."

I can still remember life before television. I knew what TV could do, even as a young boy. It's insidious and sedating. The average guy was about to spend the rest of his life on the couch.

"In the words of Captain Kangaroo," I said, "You can fool some of the people all of the time, and all of the people some of the time."

"Captain Kangaroo my ass," said the Mayor. "Americans are way too smart to fall for trickle-down, supply-side economics. The voters are going to see right through that hole of shit."

At the time, traditional Keynesian economic theory was under assault by the new supply side economics, a cause being championed by Ronald Reagan. The idea was that if we cut taxes on the rich, thus making the rich even richer, then the rich would be spurred to investment, and the richer the richest of the rich were, the more money would trickle down to the poor people below.

You don't get rich by letting your money trickle away, and the more money rich people have means there's less money, not more, left over for the rest of us. That's all that was wrong with supply side economics, and George Bush, in the political squabbling of the Republican nomination, put it best.

"Voodoo economics," is what Bush called it.

It was such a damning expression that the Mayor chortled in the front of the boat just thinking about it.

"I love it," he said. "Voodoo economics. Let the Republicans eat their own young. Carter is a shoo-in."

"I hope you're right," said the Duke, "But I'm going fishing anyway."

He rowed the banana boat backward into shore. I slid down the pile and jumped out to hold the raft. The Mayor reeled in his line, and we all looked up as the cry of a red-tailed hawk echoing down the canyon ended as abruptly as a slit throat.

Five hundred feet up a thousand foot cliff a prairie falcon flew in tight circles on quick flaps of narrow pointed wings. Below the darting falcon the bulky and apparently dead body of a red-tailed hawk spiraled down on blunt outstretched wings and dropped out of sight beyond the next bend in the river.

The Mayor opened the cooler and took out a beer.

"Bad day to be a hawk," he said.

"The falcon must have a nest up there in the cliff," said the Duke. "And the hawk came too close."

"Never come between a mother and her cubs," I said.

"I dated a woman with cubs," said the Mayor. "That hawk got off easy."

Juggling positions in the banana boat meant it was my turn to row. The Mayor went astern and the Duke went to the coveted bow seat just as the dry fly fishing was starting to get good, the way he'd planned it all along.

Salmon fly nymphs, once they reach shore, grow four wings and hatch into sexually mature adults. The adults are huge and clumsy, and tend to mate in egg-laying flights most often during the heat of the day. This is when dry flies will bring up even the biggest of fish.

Float your fly a foot from the bank and you'll catch some fish. Float your fly an inch from the bank and you'll catch a bunch of fish. At thirty feet the Duke can put it in a teacup, and he took three fish on three casts with a bushy orange fly called a Sofa Pillow.

"Allman Brothers."

"The Band."

"Credence."

We'd "Z" for zeroed out on politicians and I was glad to see the category go. You can only think about injustice for so long without bumming out. For the next alphabet we chose rock bands, and the discussion turned to great concerts over the years as the Duke tried to dry his fish-slimed fly.

"Credence," said the Mayor reverently. "I saw Credence. It was outside at Old Grizzly Field and it was fall and it snowed and the crowd got so cold they burned down the grandstands."

"I saw the crowd torch the grandstands, too," I said. "Except it was in Cincinnati. One of those all day and night deals with lots of bands. At about midnight Bonnie Raitt and Marshall Tucker got up and jammed with the Eagles; that's when the fire started."

I leaned into the oars, feeling it in my shoulders as the Duke turned around and looked at me.

"I was at that concert," he said.

There's a lot going on in a canyon, even if you can't see it all. Water is constantly chewing at the rocks. The deeper you go into the Smith River canyon the closer the cliffs come to the river until in places the sky directly overhead is reduced to a blue slice between towering grey ramparts. Canyons have a special feel because they're geologically active, and it's nice to take a turn at the oars because you get to look around.

When you're fishing hard you never look up from the water. You're lost in the currents, with one eye to your last cast and one to your next. All the casts that came before, you have to let them go, and there we were, 2.5-million-year-old humans imitating 300-million-year-old insects in order to catch 500-million-year-old fish.

Fish have been around for a long, long time. Fish are chordates, a body plan built around a backbone, and fish are as old as the Cambrian explosion of multicellular life that spawned all the major body plans for the animals we now see on planet Earth.

Before fish there had long been one-celled life on the planet, but life had only evolved in complexity as far as algae with its ability to colonize and oxygenate the atmosphere. Then, 500-million-years-ago, in the blink of a geologic eye, life took a giant organizational leap forward. In an unprecedented burst of evolutionary radiation nearly a hundred different multicellular body plans suddenly sprang into existence and began eating each other.

Those body plans included weird creatures built around cylinders and spheres that looked like they came from outer space and have long since gone extinct. Those body plans also included modern animals like arthropods, crustaceans and echinoderms along with chordates. Only about a quarter of all those original body plans survive today; but, here is what's amazing.

If a body plan didn't form in that first explosion of life, it never formed. To me, that's astonishing. In all the billions of species that evolved over the next 500 million years of life on Earth, in all that experimentation, in all that adaptation, in all that time, there were no new body plans.

The symphony of life is but variations on a theme.

Fish.

Amphibians.

Reptiles.

Birds.

Mammals.

Trout.

Creatures with backbones, we owe it all to that primitive chordate, *Ostracoderm*, a small fish that swam with all the other multicelled life so long ago in those warm Cambrian seas. *Ostracoderm* had a mouth but no jaw, and let's face it, you can only get so big if you can't chew.

The development of the hinged jaw was an adaptation that swept the animal kingdom. Chewing mouthparts are another of those physiological advantages so complete they've never really been improved upon. It's humbling, really, when you consider that a regular guy like the Mayor could represent the pinnacle of so much evolution.

"Watch this," he said.

Since last year, at the bottom of a canyon draw, there was a house where there had never been a house before. It was more of a shack really, and came complete with a flock of pecking chickens along the river bank.

Some fly-fishermen frown on wildlife casting but not the Mayor. He grew up in Montana where wildlife casting is a birthright. The Mayor throws at anything that walks, flies, or slithers, and chickens merit a category all their own.

Chickens are special because they eat insects. You can fair hook a chicken, and chickens can be as selective as trout. A beetle won't work when they're eating grasshoppers.

Wildlife casting is fun because it's challenging. Cows, for example, are almost solid leather. You can only set the hook in a couple of body parts. The soft ear tissue or the ball of hair at the end of the tail are ideal targets, but that cow is running. It's a tough cast.

The fact that you don't get one at first only makes you try harder. When you finally hook an ear or a tail and line screams from the reel as a thousand pound Angus bull stampedes through the sagebrush, that feeling, it's like heroin.

Addicting.

You'll want more. Sheep are easy, like hooking cotton. You can even get them on dry flies. A hooked badger will attack the boat and beaver are tarpon-strong. Rattlesnakes add a whole new dimension to catch-and-release fishing, but chickens, chickens are the best.

Chickens are tough.

I pulled back on the oars, holding the boat against the current as the Mayor made a good cast from sixty feet. He put his imitation salmon fly dead on those chickens, and the air was full of salmon flies. The chickens had to be eating salmon flies, but the flock of pecking Rhode-Island Reds ignored the Mayor's Sofa Pillow as they strutted up and down and all around the fly.

"Twitch it," suggested the Duke.

The Mayor twitched, a chicken pounced.

The hook plunged into the cartilage of the chicken's hinged jaw. At the bite of steel the bird went high and to the left. The Mayor yanked down hard and to the right with leverage and opposing thumbs on his side. The chicken had time for one strangled yelp before it was yanked from the air and swung like a rock on a string head first into the river.

A wet chicken is a mad chicken and this chicken was plenty mad as we dragged it squawking and flopping down the river through a rapid full of rocks. Chickens (even mad ones) aren't much at swimming, and after a quick one-sided fight the Mayor had a half-drowned chicken gasping for air at the side of the banana boat.

Legally, we were now in a grey area.

"The fishing regulations don't say anything about chickens," I said, "So we know it isn't poaching."

"We know it isn't poaching," said the Mayor, "But it might be rustling."

"Nobody's come out of the shack," observed the Duke.

What bothered us most was the inexorable progress the shack represented, so we decided to eat the evidence, and later that night the sizzling chicken spat fat as it roasted whole over an open driftwood fire.

The chicken was skewered on a spit improvised from long-handled metal barbecue tools wired together with twist ties, the make-shift spit was propped up on two forked sticks.

Beneath the chicken a fitful wind blew orange burning embers and yellow sparks off the top of the flames toward the black swooping bats over the river.

At dusk it was already cold enough that I kept my thin cheeks backed up to the fire. The bottom of a deep canyon is about as black as night gets, and by the time we licked the grease from our fingers the only light around was the faint yellow glow as we huddled around the blue campfire flames.

Campfires are nice but they only cook one side at a time. They in no way compare to the all-over glow that is the close warmth of a thick, down sleeping bag at the end of a cold day. It's like going back to the womb, and just the thought of it made me yawn.

When I yawned, so did the Mayor. That made the Duke yawn, then we all yawned together.

"Catching a hundred fish is hard work," said the Duke.

"And one chicken," said the Mayor.

Nobody even laughed.

Then we all yawned again.

After not sleeping the previous night we were in bed early our first night on the river. The initial warm bliss that is crawling into a sleeping bag, no matter how many times you've experienced it, gets better each time. I slept like a dead man, but my bones never have held the heat.

I woke up cold before dawn, shivering, the way I always do. I burrowed deeper and closed the top of the bag over my head. The slight increase in warmth just wasn't enough to overcome the large increase in sour gas.

I stuck my head back outside the bag. Crystals of frozen breath fell on my face as I exhaled. The ground gets harder by the instant in those early morning hours, so my hip bone was happy when my nose smelled coffee.

Somebody was already up.

I put on long underwear, jeans, three wool shirts, a down vest and turned on my headlamp before I zipped open the tent. It had snowed during the night, and I stomped my feet for warmth over toward where the Duke was boiling coffee on the rekindled fire.

"It snowed," I said rhetorically.

The ground, the trees, the tent, the camp; everything in the round gleam of my headlamp was covered with a half-inch of powdery snow. The Duke laughed hysterically.

"It isn't snow," he said.

I reached down and scraped a fistful off the ground. It wasn't snow because it wasn't wet. It was too dry and dusty to be snow. Plus, when you really looked, it wasn't white either. There was some grey in it, and some yellow.

"What is this stuff?" I wondered out loud.

Tears ran down his cheeks, and the Duke's pupils were the size of dimes in the soft glow of the low fire.

"What is it?" he said. "It's World War Three."

Not for one instant did I doubt that life as we knew it had just ended in a fall of radioactive ash. Ronald Reagan had been all over the news lately promising to get tough on Communism, and I just figured the Soviets were making a preemptive strike.

You have to understand. We grew up during the height of America's Cold War against the Red menace of Communism. As children, we were taught to expect Armageddon. We did drills in school where they made us hide under our desks. The question wasn't if the commies were coming, it was when.

At the time, Montana was the world's fourth largest atomic power. Minuteman missile silos speckled the wheat and sagebrush plains. It was no secret that we'd be hit hard and we'd be hit early, and the Duke was sanguine as we watched pulverized Paradise sift down like flour from the sky.

"How long do you think we have?" he asked.

The sky was falling fast enough to coat my upturned palm with grit in the glow of my headlamp. In Hiroshima, radiation burns appeared within hours of exposure. We wouldn't live long enough to watch our hair fall out.

"A day," I said, "Maybe two."

I watched as the Duke mixed dried blue mushrooms and Swiss cheese into the stirred eggs that would later become an omelet. I didn't know how to feel about the end of the world. At first I was sad, then I was mad, and then I thought, what the hell, it isn't like this is the first time.

Multicellular life on Earth has gone through five major mass extinctions in the last half-billion years, and many scientists believed that even without the exclamation point of nuclear war, we were teetering on the brink of the sixth major mass extinction of life on Earth.

Two hundred years into the industrial age species are disappearing at a rate the world hasn't seen since the end of the trilobites. Not even the dinosaurs died off as fast as species are now. The only comparable death rate seems to be about 245-million-years-ago, during the Permian "mother of all mass extinctions," when life on Earth had its closest brush with total death.

At the time, devastating ice ages gripped the land, which lowered sea levels. Rotting organic matter on the exposed continental shelves may have reduced atmospheric oxygen inducing death by suffocation. The continents had drifted together to form the supercontinent Pangaea, which had the effect of reducing available habitat. Whatever the cause, an estimated ninety-five percent of marine species died off during the Permian extinction, never to be seen again.

The important thing was that after each of these five mass extinction events, life bounced back. Darwin viewed evolution as a slow, smooth process, but current theory holds that life lurches along in fits and bursts, recovering from one catastrophe only to encounter another.

It was a theory I could get behind because it so much resembled the ups and downs of my own life.

"Is that for me?" I asked.

I pointed at the omelet the Duke had been making. He smiled back with square chipped teeth that glowed amber in the eerie light of the radioactive dawn.

"It is if you want it to be," he replied.

Mushroom and Swiss, even smothered with ketchup the steaming omelet was so dry it turned cold on the tin plate before I finished it. The Mayor was standing off to the side peeing, his dick in one hand, and a beer in the other hand, which made it tough when he sneezed.

"This dust," he said back over his shoulder, "Is going to play hell with my allergies."

It was like breathing talcum powder driven by a cold wind that scraped deep into the sinus cavities. The sun was up but daylight in the dust storm never came. The air was yellow and it got more yellow as the Duke poured another omelet into the skillet.

"What do you think is going to happen?" he said.

"You know what I think," I said. ". . . It's complicated."

Sometimes I get the feeling even my friends think I'm a crackpot, it's just that they're too nice to tell me.

"We have time," said the Mayor.

The Duke cracked a breakfast beer.

"Nothing but time," he said.

So I told them.

What I think is that at a few times in the history of the planet life has literally exploded in new directions. There wasn't anything slow about it. Carboniferous insects learned to fly in one of those explosions. One geologic instant no insects could fly, the next geologic instant many insects could fly. There were mayflies, dragonflies, stone-flies; suddenly, after only a few million years, the air was filled with flies.

The Cambrian explosion of multicellular life is another one of these events in which life took a huge, giant, quick leap forward. One geologic day the Earth was populated with one-celled algae; a couple of geologic hours later a dazzling array of multicelled life based on dozens and dozens and dozens of wildly different body plans were swimming around checking each other out.

What I think is that the enlargement of the prefrontal lobe and the development of conscious thought is the latest of these great explosions in the complexity of life. The human brain is just too much of a competitive advantage. Other species are going to want in on it.

As a fly-fisherman, I read about the history of bugs. What I couldn't understand was how so many different aquatic insects would start flying at the same time. It happened so fast. One bug learning to fly, that I could understand. But how could a whole menagerie of bugs take to the lightning-filled skies of the Carboniferous en masse?

Here's what else I think:

You are what you eat.

If one insect learned to fly, that ability would be encoded in its genes. If a second insect ate the first insect, it's easy to see how that fresh raw genetic code could become absorbed in the cells of the second insect. The insects that learned to fly were the insects that were eating each other as nymphs at the bottom of the Carboniferous swamps.

Cell biologists now know genes can be passed not just within a species, but between species. Genes can pass not just cat to cat, but cat to dog. But so what? A dog doesn't need to be a cat. Not unless the cat has wings.

Or the cat is really smart.

When an adaptation is so novel, so overwhelming, it's going to spill over. It's going to take life in a new direction. The genetic information that leads to conscious thought is out there on the loose. Other species are going to pick up on it.

"So what you're saying," said the Mayor, "Is that birds are going to get brains. Interesting . . . "

"Radiation is a wild card," said the Duke. "It could just as easy be worms that are going to get arms."

"If worms get arms," said the Mayor, "I hope they can hit the curve ball better than the bunch of bums they got playing for the Braves now."

The Duke slid an omelet onto the upturned Frisbee the Mayor was using as a plate; the Mayor picked up a fork and pointed it at me.

"If you think about it," he said. "Your theory is kind of like reincarnation. Life passing on and the spirit that is in all of us and the rest of that Holy Ghost shit."

"Maybe," I said. "I never thought of it like that."

The Duke, as he cooked, kept looking over his shoulder into the gloom like something was out there.

"Maybe it's already happening," he said. "Maybe animals are getting smarter already."

"Look at dolphins," said the Mayor. "I've watched them hunt in packs. They're definitely communicating, you know, making plans together."

The way the Duke couldn't stop looking back into the darkness was starting to make me nervous.

"What's up?" I said. "Do you hear something?"

The Duke hates spiders so much; it probably stems from some childhood trauma.

"Spiders with brains. I'm not so sure I like that idea," said the Duke.

Standing around the burning driftwood logs in the yellow darkness, giant smart spiders weren't something I wanted to think about either. I had a prickly feeling in the base of my neck that I was being watched the whole time as we broke down camp, and even though we were going fishing it was tough leaving the safe glow of the warm campfire.

The bottom of the canyon was freezing cold as we floated down the river with handkerchiefs tied cowboy style over our mouths and noses to keep out the choking dust. The Mayor's raft was bright yellow to begin with, now it glowed like neon mustard spread over olive water beneath a soupy golden sky that fairly reeked of fornication.

Violet-green swallows and black nighthawks sliced the silent dust as we floated. The false twilight had triggered biological clocks throughout the food chain. Somehow, the insects knew. Get it done now or don't get it done at all. It was time to fertilize some eggs. The sky was falling, and entire populations were going at it in a droning rustle of wings an octave above the low rumble of the river.

The dark canyon echoed with our sneezes, and the cliff walls boiled with the floating chop of hungry trout heads. Gorging fish slashed under a sky too thick with decaying protons for the sun to pierce. It was the best fishing of my life, but what I remember most is the bugs.

Salmon flies. Golden stone flies. Blue-winged Olives. Yellow Sallies. March Browns. Pale-morning duns. Insects filled the air with their delicate colors. Bugs blanketed the water, painted the boat, crawled down your neck, tickled your arms, scuttled through the hair on your chest. It would have been creepy if the colors hadn't been so amazing.

"Wow," I said.

Insects breathe by diffusion through pores in their shells, and the more oxygen in the atmosphere, the larger the insects can grow. Carboniferous oxygen levels were nearly twice what they are today, and floating along in the looming shadow of the Madison limestone, it was easy to imagine that long-ago time when mayflies the size of canaries were dodging dragonflies the size of eagles.

I couldn't take my eyes off the frantic insect mélange on my arm when I was suddenly pitched forward off my seat as the banana boat stopped dead on a rock in the middle of the river. I picked myself up off the floor of the raft and settled back into the middle seat.

"Who's rowing this thing anyway?" I asked.

"You are," replied the Mayor.

I looked down at the wooden oars in my hands.

"That's what I was afraid of," I replied.

"If you think this is going to get you out of rowing," said the Duke, "Forget it."

I looked around, sizing up my options. We were hard aground on a barely submerged boulder in the middle of a rapid. To the left, there was deep rushing water. To the right, there was deep rushing water.

"Let's camp here," I said.

Considering the fact that the world was coming to an end, I didn't feel all that badly. As a matter of fact, I felt great. My jaw hurt I'd been smiling so much, and as long as we were going nowhere fast the Mayor tossed a cast into the eddy below the next rock over.

He hooked a golden-bellied trout that jumped seven times before it got away. Behind me on top of the pyramid of gear the Duke played in a big brown with jaws that met in a curve like a goofy smile. The fish taped out at twenty-four inches, and the Duke slid it over the side with this advice:

"Never eat anything bigger than your head."

It should have been sobering, knowing we were dying, but we were too young for proper introspection. All we'd ever done was drink beer, chase women, and catch fish.

What was there to regret?

On the off chance we were headed for Heaven we decided it would be best if we didn't show up with any gin.

When you've partied like there's no tomorrow and tomorrow comes, you're not going to feel very well, not when you're jolted from your dream-torn stupor by terrified screams.

"A bear," the Duke was screaming. "A bear."

I opened gummy eye-lids just far enough for the sun to hurt my eyes. It was the morning after and I was laying on hard river rock, using a tin plate for a pillow. A small black bear was crouched over the Mayor, eating his face.

"Eating his face!"

My eyelashes ripped open the rest of the way.

It's not every friend that will charge a bear, and the Duke was up and running like the linebacker he once was. His stout legs churned, but he'd forgotten his brown neoprene waders, which were pulled down to his knees. The Duke tripped over the waders and went down like he'd been chain-sawed, pitching head first into a cottonwood sapling and knocking himself unconscious at the dog's feet.

Dog?

I blinked at the power of suggestion. I'd heard bear, I'd seen bear, but it wasn't a bear at all. It was a black Labrador retriever, and it wasn't eating the Mayor, it was eating the plate of beans on the ground next to his head.

"Ell . . . mer . . ."

A little girl's thin reedy voice floated on the bright air. Elmer the dog knew his name, and his black hairy snout rose up from the beans at the call. I sat up and checked; there was a red raft on the beach next to the banana boat.

We had company in the wilderness, and a young girl appeared, her blonde pigtails swinging beside pink cheeks under a blue ski cap. Wind had blown the radioactive dust into dunes, and the girl was scooping the powder into a green plastic beach bucket with a matching plastic shovel.

"You should be careful," I said. "That ash is dangerous."

The little girl looked at me with sad green eyes that said I was pathetic, even for an adult.

"It's just volcano dust," she said. "Daddy says we're gonna sell it to the tourists."

Entire philosophic disciplines are dedicated to the idea that man makes his own reality and I guess I'm the evidence. The possibility of a Mount Saint Helens explosion had been in the news. I was just so sure the world was ending that I'd forgotten, and I was feeling kind of foolish as the Mayor woke up with Elmer licking at his face.

"Hey, there, boy," said the Mayor as he sat up and scratched Elmer between the eyes.

"All this ash," I explained to the Mayor. "It was Mount Saint Helens."

The Mayor looked at me like his head hurt.

"You didn't know that?" he said.

And now in the rocks, whenever I wander by the white tuff that is the frozen ash flow of some ancient volcano, I can't help but wonder how good the fishing must have been back when mayflies were the size of canaries.

"Of course I knew that," I replied.

DANCES WITH SHARKS

On Redcoat Key, a desert island at the edge of the Gulf Stream, a bay is a bight and a creek is part of the ocean. Cars have bonnets, kissing cousins do more than just kiss, and Half-Moon Harbor on the west side of the island is renowned throughout the Caribbean as a haven in a hurricane.

The sheltered anchorage draws sailors from the world over, and was settled by hard-scrabble English Loyalists forced to flee the United States after the American Revolution. All the old local names are either Scottish or Irish, and the Bight of Old MacTavish is a crescent-shaped bay spotted with orange coral heads, surrounded by mangroves, and home to the kind of bonefish that can haunt your dreams.

I wake up, sweating, in the middle of the night, as wet as the fish that swim through my sleep. Heart racing, what I can't forget are the ones that got away.

MacTavish bonefish are tough. They can see, hear, and smell you coming. They spook at a single false cast. When you finally do get a fly to the fish, they'll sniff but they won't eat. It can be maddening, but the best things in life don't come free.

You work for them, and one cloudy afternoon I was easing along the hard-bottomed White Sand Flat at the north end of the bight. A tiny mushroom of sand was puffing up with each deliberate step of my rubber flats booties, and the tide was falling hard when three of the biggest bonefish I'd ever seen meandered out of a patch of turtle grass. The fish were so big at first I thought they were barracuda, and they were coming straight for me.

It couldn't have been any easier. All I had to do was stand still and make a cast. I put a crab fly in front of the approaching bonefish, let the fly sink to the hard sand bottom, and then twitched the artificial fly like a real crab trying to bury itself in the bottom when the fish arrived. A bonefish as fat as a silver watermelon followed my slithering fly through the sand all the way to the rod tip before spooking at my feet.

The bonefish was interested, but wouldn't eat.

Why?

"I still think it's the way the fly smells," I said.

"This time," said Bean. "Let's really make a stink box."

"OK," said Montana, "Who's going to get the crabs?"

Montana's lush grey beard grows from the middle of his chest to his eyebrows. He looks kind of like an aging Yeti, if the Yeti was waking up in Ohio after his buddies got him drunk and put him on a bus. Jolly Bean, with his white beard and red nose, looks more like Santa Claus.

"Who has the crabs?" he said.

At the end of a long day on the flats, we were sitting around on the deck at the Sea Horse, the house we were renting in Half-Moon Harbor. The wind was coming in off the ocean at a steady twenty knots, and it wasn't the first time we'd talked about making up a stink box.

The idea was simple enough, an airtight plastic container containing a few favored flies and a chunk of dead crab meat. At the very least the smell of the fermenting crab would help mask human odors like sweat and suntan lotion; at best the crab juice would provoke strikes. It was a sensible idea we all agreed, the problem was crab procurement.

Those little suckers are fast.

It was a lot easier to sit in a big chair with your feet up on the railing of the deck overlooking the blue Atlantic Ocean than it was to run down a crab. It had been a hard day of fishing. I wasn't sure I could get up, much less bend over.

"Maybe if we got a net," I said.

Everybody on Redcoat Key has a nickname. There's Electric Bill, Walking Stick Mike, Delirious Dave, Bongo Bob, the Dick Whisperer; Tiny is Tiny because he's so big.

"You Yankees is way too old to be running down fiddler crabs," said Tiny. "Instead of bringing the boy to the crab, what we'll do is bring the crab to the boy, if you know what I mean. We'll chum us up some hermit crabs. Y'all with me?"

"Chumming," said Montana," I'm with you."

Tiny's laugh rumbled up from a barrel-sized chest covered in a T-shirt that said "Beer is Food." He'd just torn out his knee falling from the top to the bottom of his sailboat, so Tiny was limping as he went down the stairs from the grey wooden deck to the green and yellow spike-grass lawn.

The Sea Horse is Tiny's rental-by-the-sea. It was supposed to be the Sea House, but the original sign painter got the spelling wrong. It's been the Sea Horse ever since, and at the bottom of the deck stairs there's a tilted table under a plywood shed roof where Tiny keeps some essentials handy.

"You want crabs," he said. "Then coconuts is the secret ingredient. Them hermit crabs can't get enough of them coconuts. You'd think them crabs was lonely Montana boys and that coconut was a piece of ass the way they go after it.

"Just let me get my cutlass, here."

Redcoat Key has a recent enough pirate heritage that a machete is called a cutlass, and with two swings of his meaty arm Tiny had sliced the end a big green coconut down to the top end of the hairy brown seed inside. Four more strategically placed whacks and the hard seed case was free. Tiny threw the chopped copra husk out on to the bristly lawn for the crabs, then picked another coconut from the pile.

"Might as well whack us up a couple, three," he said. "I think I'll cook us up some coconut grouper tonight. How does that sound, boys?"

It sounded damn good. Tiny cooks sea food with skill and originality. The best fish I've ever eaten has come out of the sprawling kitchen at the back of the Sea Horse. It wasn't much past six but it was already pushing dusk when a fuzzy moth the size of a hummingbird fluttered out of the gathering darkness and tried to nest in my hair.

"What the hell kind of bug is that?" Montana asked.

Tiny looked up from where he was liberating coconuts to where I was leaping back and forth swatting at the moth.

"That there is what the Haitians call a gypsy death moth," said Tiny.

"Because they're poisonous?" asked Bean.

"No, mon," said Tiny. "Because they're Voodoo."

The moth had a proboscis as long as its body, and the way it was dogging me and only me, it wasn't natural. No matter where I went on the deck, the moth followed.

"Voodoo?" I said.

"Yah, mon," said Tiny. "The Haitians believe that there moth is a sign of bad luck, maybe even death; sure is a hell of a moth though, any bug could make a Yankee dance like that."

It was a good moment to break the news.

"Attacked by a gypsy death moth," I could have said. "That reminds me, I have cancer."

I could have said something, but I didn't. I went inside to get away from the moth instead. It's tough finding the right time to tell people you have cancer. The longer you put it off, the harder it gets, and I never did get around to it that night.

I slept fitfully, and if the Bight of Old MacTavish haunted my dreams, so did the rubber dinghy. Anybody who has ever been lost at sea can relate, and the following morning Bean kicked at the limp grey ring of the uninflated dinghy.

"I've seen more air in a donut," he said.

We were ready to go fishing, hoping we'd have the use of the dinghy, and Montana's brown eyes blinked from deep within his bushy grey beard.

"At least you can eat a donut," he said.

The flaccid dinghy lay on the dirty sand at the back end of Half-Moon Harbor, near the twisted plank-and-piling dock lined with sail boats and motor yachts swaying at anchor.

"Don't you Yankees worry," said Tiny, "We got her licked this time."

The problem was the foot pump, which Tiny held in his ham-sized paws.

"Domino, domino, palomino," I said, blessing the pump.

The chrome ring holding the thin plastic bellows on the wooden foot pad had broken. Tiny had tried twice to fix it, first with wraps of heavy monofilament, and now with wraps of monofilament reinforced with duct tape. The first repair hadn't worked at all, but Tiny was optimistic as he inserted the pump's black plastic hose into the dinghy's air valve.

"Duct tape," he said. "The only thing it can't cure is a broken heart or a hangover."

Montana held up a can of cold Budweiser.

"It's science," he said. "But it works like magic."

Tiny stepped on the pump with his flat barefoot and air hissed into the dinghy. I hadn't realized I was holding my breath until I let it out. The repair was working, and one of the dinghy's two tubes was beginning to take shape.

"Now," said Bean, "If only it holds air."

"Hold air?" said Tiny. "This dinghy has been around the world on the back of my sailboat. This dinghy will be holding air long after we're all dead and gone. This dinghy will . . ."

The pump wheezed like a broken bagpipe as the bladder again separated from the bellows.

"I might beat the dinghy to the grave," said Montana, "But I'm thinking I've already outlasted that pump."

Tiny growled and with one swift kick sent the pump flying into the waves.

"Damn it boys," he said, "They sure don't make duct tape like they used to."

Montana finished his beer, lit an unfiltered Camel cigarette with a tarnished Zippo lighter, and then waded into the water to retrieve the soggy pump.

"Tonight," he said, "I'm fixing this once and for all."

We all stood around in the wind.

"Well . . . ," said Bean.

I put the trip together, the dinghy was part of the deal, and I felt guilty even though nobody was blaming me.

"I'm going to O'Brien's," I said.

The previous afternoon I'd seen the three giant bonefish on the White Sand Flat, but those were the only fish I'd seen. O'Brien's Creek is the flat that most consistently holds fish in the Bight of Old MacTavish; that's where I was going.

"No worries mon," said Tiny. "I'll haul you over in *Guido*, drop you off wherever you want to fish."

Guido is another of Tiny's many boats, a heavy V-hulled Boston Whaler. It draws too much water for proper flats fishing, but until the dinghy was operational, Tiny had been using the whaler to ferry us back and forth to the bight.

"The White Sand Flat for me," said Montana.

Bean took off his Cleveland Indians ball cap and ran a hand through the wispy hair up top. The wading is a lot easier in the sand, and he decided he'd go with Montana.

"All right then," I said. "I'm just going to walk over to O'Brien's. I'll see you later."

"Walk?" said Tiny. "At least let me give you a ride."

"I said I'd walk," I snapped.

The only sound was the putt of an outboard motor out in the harbor until Bean cleared his throat.

"Are you OK?" he said.

"I'm fine," I lied.

"Then how come you're crying?"

"Because I'm so glad to see you," I said.

I left the three of them shaking their heads on the beach beside the dinghy and started down a road lumpy with limestone shelf rock. The word was out on Half-Moon Harbor.

Five years earlier there had been a couple dozen houses, now there were a couple hundred, and the land on either side of me was increasing in value by the minute.

The blue realtor's sign on the lot at the top of the rise that said "For Sale" yesterday had been marked "Sold" today, and the new owners had already hired a bare-chested man of muscled ebony to clear-cut the land with a cutlass.

If you see a black man doing manual labor in the islands it's a good bet he's from Haiti. Haiti is the poorest country in the Caribbean, and Haitians seeking work in other countries are treated like slaves. Clearing jungle with a knife is long hard work and the man was cutting the tedium with a long white joint.

"Spleef, mon?" he said, waving the joint in invitation with his left hand as he hacked with the right.

"No, thanks," I said, "Water?"

The man whistled appreciatively as I pulled a bottle of water still cold from the refrigerator. Where twenty years ago there were desert islands fit more for lizards than men, now there was bottled water, nicely chilled.

"Oh, tank you mon," he said.

We introduced ourselves. His name was Toussaint, and he kept one eye closed as he examined my gear.

"So I suspects dat be's a fishing rod," he said, "But what kind, never mind."

"It's a fly rod," I said. "You use it for bonefish."

Toussaint whistled appreciatively and rubbed his flat rippled stomach.

"Dem bonefish," he said, "Dey eat some good come dinner time, de big ones mostly."

The Haitians on Redcoat Key live on a mixed bag of whatever fish turns up in the shanty town. The fish generally come from illegal nets and are sold by the burlap sack, twenty-five dollars a bag, all guts included, and no questions asked.

"How big?" I asked. "The bonefish, I mean."

"Oh, beeg," he said, "Eight, could be nine kilos."

A nine kilo bonefish would be as large as any ever recorded. That world-record bonefish still existed was encouraging, that such valuable sport fish were being netted and sold for chowder made me want to scream at the insanity.

"Can I tell you something?" I said.

His palm showed white as Toussaint wiped his lips with the back of his hand.

"Sure ting," he said. "Tells away."

"I have cancer."

There. It was out. Somehow it was easier to tell this man who was so black he was almost purple, someone I'd never met before in my life.

"Where at is dis sickness?" he asked.

I knew talking would be hard, but this was even harder than I thought. My larynx was so tight I could barely speak.

"The prostate," I choked out.

Toussaint looked at the joint, then looked back at me. The way I figured it, I couldn't feel much worse.

"Ah, what the hell," I said.

We stood there a while, not long, but long enough that a purple orchid with red spots on thick lipped petals blossomed right before our very eyes. Light was flooding the heretofore dark jungle at the end of Toussaint's cutlass, and I think that orchid bloomed because it could tell the end was near. If a local plant was that smart, it made me wonder about the neighborhood bugs, and I turned to Toussaint.

"What do you know about gypsy death moths?" I asked.

A visible shudder went through Toussaint from the scalp down as he fingered a wooden totem on a thong at his throat.

"Why you ask?" he said.

"I saw one last night," I said. "It wouldn't leave me alone. It just kept coming back."

The whites of Toussaint's eyes were big and round as Ping-Pong balls.

"It no land on you," he said. "Tell me dat."

In the darkness before dawn I'd woken from a patch of fitful sleep with the moth perched on the bridge of my nose. It was my turn to shudder at the memory of the flutter of soft gooey body hair.

"Kind of," I said. "Maybe a little."

Toussaint leaned in close, his breath fresh as vegetables.

"Was de moth grey?" he asked.

"Yes."

"With de shape of a skull on de wings?"

"Yes."

Toussaint dropped his chin to his chest.

"Dat de worst kind," he said.

Toussaint was so obviously terrified that it was catching. Goose bumps rose on the back of my neck.

"What do I do?" I asked.

The idea of a white man who believed in voodoo was not an opportunity Toussaint could pass up, because he leaned in closer and closer until the short curly hair on his bare chest scraped like wires on my arm.

"Best you bites de head off a chicken," he said.

And then he started to giggle. Which made me start to giggle. I felt better than I had in weeks as Toussaint, cutlass in hand, turned back to the wall of jungle before him.

"You bush," he said, "You in for some beating now."

And then he laughed and laughed. Pretty soon I joined in. After all, as I continued down the limestone road that led into the Bight of Old MacTavish, the joke was on me.

There had never been any cancer in my family history, none at all. I didn't have any symptoms, but I was turning fifty, so I'd gone in for a routine physical, the one where they do the digital rectal exam.

Now there's a euphemism.

"Hey, Doc, why don't you use a couple of fingers, get a second opinion?"

In retrospect the vigor of the examination was my first clue. The doctor was just making sure as he shoved me all over the table like an apple on a stick. When it was finally over I saw the news in the doctor's bleak eyes even before he removed the purple latex gloves.

"There's a lump in your prostate," he said.

At that point what I knew about a prostate would fit on the end of a finger.

"What is a prostate anyway?" I asked.

The prostate is a walnut sized gland that manufactures most of the fluid that keeps the sperm alive during the sperm's journey to the egg. Sperm plus fluid is called semen, and it's terribly sticky stuff, so the chemical plant that is the prostate also produces an enzyme that thins the semen allowing the sperm to swim freely once they reach the promised land.

This enzyme is called Prostate Specific Antigen, or PSA. There's always some of it in a man's body, but too much PSA in the circulatory system means something is amiss with the plumbing. A simple blood test for PSA delivers a standardized number. Anything over four is bad, anything over ten is really bad; mine was fourteen.

Even at this point the news wasn't good, but it wasn't necessarily bad. The PSA could be elevated due to an infection. The lump in my prostate could be benign. The chances that I had cancer were still only about fifty-fifty; the only way to know for sure was to remove some prostate cells for biopsy.

Access to the prostate is through the butt, and the various fingers that had been diddling in my nether regions were a walk in the park compared to the posthole digger that came next.

The biopsy is guided by ultrasound, which means your prostate is displayed on a video screen as core samples are taken with specialized needles that snap like alligators at the end of a hollow plastic probe the size of a giant white cucumber.

While you're still awake.

The alligator snapped twelve times in all, sampling my prostate, up, down and all around. The tissue was then sent off to a lab for pathological cell analysis, but the lab was closed for the Thanksgiving holiday. I was stymied at every turn.

I hated the idea that a cancer might be growing inside me as I waited, but what with one delay after another it had been twenty-eight days exactly since the lump was first discovered before the doctor's secretary called and said the results were back from the lab.

I knew as soon as she asked me to come to the office.

If it's good news, the doctor tells you over the phone. If it's bad news, he tells you to your face. It was cancer, but it didn't have to be the end of the world. At my age, with no cancer in the family, the chances were still good that the tumor was small and treatable as I sat down in front of the books and papers piled on the doctor's messy desk.

"So," I said, "How bad is it?"

The noose around my neck tightened with every word out of his mouth.

"Bad," he said.

Twelve out of twelve core samples taken from my prostate were positive. The cancer was aggressive, undifferentiated, and high-volume. It was all the stuff you don't want to hear, a worst-case scenario, and the doctor recommended surgery.

"What are my chances of beating this cancer?" I asked.

My eyes were so wet I could barely make the doctor out.

"With surgery," he said, "There's an eighty percent chance this cancer will be back in two years."

"Two years!" I said.

"At which point," he said, "You can pursue a course of radiation therapy."

Surgery now and radiation in two years. Over the last month, at every step in the process, the news couldn't have been worse. It was unbelievable. The tears gushing down my cheeks were so salty they tasted like blood.

"About the surg . . . surg . . ."

I tried to say surgery and couldn't get it out. My body isn't like a chess match, where a pawn can be sacrificed to save the king. I hated the idea that part of me had to be cut out. I took a deep breath and held it until the screaming in my organs subsided, until my tongue could wrap itself around the question pounding on my skull.

"Can you spare the nerves?"

The nerves in question are directly adjacent to the prostate and run the local Erection Service. A skilled surgeon can take the prostate but leave the nerves. Skilled is the key word here. Figure your odds at fifty-fifty, not great, but at least you have a chance at maintaining normal function. There has to be hope, but there wasn't.

"The cancer has spread too far," the doctor said. "Your nerves have to go."

A hundred percent chance of impotence, and an eighty percent chance of dying, that's what I was hearing.

"I don't know . . . ," I said.

The doctor played with a pen on his desk, looking to the side as he ran through the other options and why he didn't recommend them.

"External radiation is generally insufficient to eliminate the malignancy at its original focus," he said, "And when the tumor grows back the implications in your day-to-day existence are severe." Then he shuddered. "As a urologist I have to fix people after radiation doesn't work," he said, "And after radiation the surgery becomes much more difficult, nearly impossible, due to the amount of scarring in the prostate."

Click, click, click went the pen as the doctor pushed the metal end in and out.

"What about the radioactive seed implants?" I said. "It seems like lots of people have had success with that procedure."

The procedure in which radioactive "seeds" are placed in the prostate is called brachytherapy. It is a low-impact surgery that has the advantage of delivering a higher dose of radiation to the area of the central tumor, but it doesn't control cancer that has already spread out of the prostate, and the doctor shrugged.

"Brachytherapy has been shown to be effective against localized tumors," he said, "But again we return to the issue of post-radiation scar tissue versus the high likelihood that the prostate will eventually have to be removed in order to maintain some degree of urinary function as the disease progresses."

What he was saying was surgery now would make me more comfortable as I was dying later. But I didn't want to die, I wanted to live. The noose around my neck was all in my head but I still could barely breathe. There had to be a way out of this.

"What about radiation after the surgery?" I said.

The doctor nodded approvingly.

"You may well wish to pursue a course of external radiation one to two years after surgery," he said. "Your rising PSA will be the guide as to when the regimen should begin."

This didn't make any sense either. A rising PSA would mean the cancer had already spread and was growing somewhere else inside me. Why wait a year or two before beginning radiation? It made more sense to hit the cancer hard and hit the cancer early. The way to hit it hardest was to cut it out, but if the cancer had already grown free of the prostate it didn't make sense to cut the prostate out.

It would be like blowing up the cave after the terrorists have already left for the city; an expensive and misdirected show of power. You're occupied with the cave, meanwhile the bad guys are loose in the city where they can really do some damage. On the other hand, new terrorists might come back to the old cave. It was all too much and my brain was beginning to shut down. I sat there crying hard enough that the chest of my shirt was wet and we hadn't even talked about turning a woman loose inside my body yet.

"What about . . . hormone . . . therapy?" I said between sobs. "From what . . . I've read . . . it seems to help."

Prostate cancer in men, like breast cancer in women, is hormone driven. Breast cancer feeds on estrogen, prostate cancer feeds on testosterone, and depriving either cancer of its food can help slow the cancer growth. In some men testosterone deprivation therapy can even temporarily shrink the tumor.

The Achilles' heel of hormone therapy is that some prostate cancer cells do just fine in the absence of testosterone. Hormone therapy can't cure prostate cancer, only slow it down, and the doctor shrugged again, obviously uninterested.

"Hormone therapy renders the prostate margin indistinct," he said. "If you choose to undergo hormone therapy then surgery would be delayed six to eight months until the prostate margins redefine."

More waiting. I didn't want to wait six months before surgery, not when the hormone-resistant cancer cells could be riding the highway of lymph nodes toward my spine, because once prostate cancer metastasizes to the spine, there's not much left to do but make out your will.

At least that would be easy.

"And of course," continued the doctor, "You're aware of the side effects of the hormone therapy?"

On this point my reading had been quite clear.

"All too aware," I replied.

At a certain point in their lives women naturally quit making estrogen, and the variety of associated symptoms is called menopause. Artificially depriving a man of testosterone induces the same menopausal symptoms. If I began hormone therapy, I'd be a man trapped in a woman's body.

"If I had the surgery," I asked, " Whu-whu-when?"

The doctor looked at his calendar.

"Thursday would be good," he said.

The urethra, the tube through which urine passes, runs right through the middle of the prostate. Removing the prostate means severing the urethra, which means peeing into a bag on your hip until the urethra can be hooked up again, which means another surgery. The bladder, the rectum, the seminal vesicles, a plethora of veins, arteries, nerves; the prostate is right in the middle of all that plumbing. Cutting it out isn't easy.

Complications are real, and some men never get better.

I could end up peeing into a bag for the rest of my unnatural life. The truth is, I wasn't sure I wanted to live like that at all, much less beginning the next Thursday.

"No offense," I said, "But I'm getting a second opinion."

I did get a second opinion, and a third, fourth, fifth, and sixth. Every doctor had something different to say. I was drowning in conflicting information and none of it was promising. I was leaning toward radiation because there was less of a chance I'd end up impotent in a diaper, but before ruling out surgery I wanted to talk to a man who was good with the scalpel.

I wanted a top-dog surgeon, somebody who had removed thousands of prostates. I wanted a recognized expert in the field, so I decided to spend the money to seek out a center of excellence. I went to a teaching hospital to see the man they call Doctor Knife, and all I can say is let the buyer beware.

First off, I was an emotional basket case. It took three weeks to even see Doctor Knife. My appointment was for 7:30 A.M., two days before Christmas, and I hadn't slept more than two hours in a row since the biopsies had come back positive at Thanksgiving. Since then I'd talked to six doctors and read four books on the subject. I had a hundred questions all jumbling around in my brain, about fifty of them dealing with impotence.

"What about it, Doc, can you take the prostate but spare the nerves? Is there anything that you, as a very skilled surgeon in a hospital with all the best equipment, can do better?"

"I've heard about this nerve graft procedure, where they take a nerve from your leg and splice it in after the fact. Is that snake oil, or does it work?"

I had a hundred questions, and one gut feeling.

In retrospect, the eighteen previous months had been something else. I'd always been horny but not like that. It was like I was crazed, a period of what now seemed almost like a possession and coincided eerily with the exponential growth of my cancer. It felt to me like my cancer really liked its testosterone, and maybe even as a colony was able to demand it.

I saw my cancer as a smart plant, a plant that could send chemical messages, a plant with a chemical habit. Taking away the testosterone, I thought, would make this cancer suffer.

I knew I would.

My gut feeling was that hormone therapy should be part of my treatment. If I opted for hormones, then radiation was the next logical step, because six months was too long to wait for surgery, which meant there was a high probability the cancer would return at the original source of the tumor, which meant more questions for Doctor Knife.

"What about it, Doc, how hard is it to take out a radiated prostate after the scar tissue has formed? Is this something that you, as a surgeon who knows all the tricks, can do, or is surgery after radiation something to be avoided at all costs?"

"Is it true you have to wait six months after starting hormone therapy to do surgery? Is there any way around that?"

"What about chemotherapy? How come nobody has had much luck with chemotherapy of prostate cancer? They do chemotherapy on breast cancer."

"If I was your dad, what would you tell him to do?"

"Did you and your dad get along?"

I had another question for Doctor Knife. I wanted to ask him if he did the surgery himself or if he just supervised it. I'd heard scuttlebutt that in teaching hospitals you don't always get the expert. You could get a resident-in-training and the last thing I wanted was a newbie with a knife.

I had dozens of questions and a tape recorder to help remember exactly what the doctor said. I arrived at 7:00

for a 7:30 appointment and had been awake since midnight. It seemed like years since I'd slept. At Doctor Knife's office the coffee wasn't even going yet. It was coming on Christmas so I understood. Everybody had lots to do. My cancer wasn't convenient.

I sat in a black leather and chrome chair reading the paper until about a quarter to eight, when I was summoned by a nurse with the demeanor of a drill sergeant. She marched me to yet another in a long line of stark white examination rooms with florescent lighting. I sat in there a while, waiting, listening to the lights buzz, just waiting.

After a time Doctor Knife breezed in. He seemed like a nice-enough guy; tall, slender, and tanned with a mouth full of bleached teeth. He had a ready smile, a surfer-boy grin as he introduced himself and picked up my file. After a silence that drew out he said:

"Hmmm."

Another silence stretched as he studied my file; finally he looked up, still smiling.

"Hmmm . . . ," he said. "I see you're from Montana."

Doctor Knife didn't even know I'd traveled eight hundred miles to see him. The conclusion was as disappointing as it was obvious.

"Is this the first time you've looked at my file?" I said.

The sunny smile faded to a grin.

"Busy, busy," he said. "Busy, busy. Now bend over."

All the doctors so far were just as busy but they had all somehow managed to find the time to stick a cold finger up my ass. It's like they didn't trust all the cold fingers that came before. This latest and I hoped last was not only cold but long and thin with a knobby knuckle.

"Yes," it concurred, "That lump in your prostate sure is big and hard."

Doctor Knife threw the used latex glove in a white metal wastebasket. He looked at his big gold watch, gave me a napkin to wipe the jellied lubricant off my butt, and then spent five minutes talking himself through to a conclusion, which was that my cancer was actually worse than anybody had thought.

"Hmmm . . . ," he said. "Yes, I think we safely assume a Gleason score of nine, which would qualify you nicely for ongoing study XYX AB 40, but let me see, probably not AB 98 4,000 . . ."

All those numbers; it sounded like he was calling a football play. He went on and on but what kept ringing in my ears was a Gleason of nine.

The Gleason score is a measure of the grade of the cancer, or how aggressively the cancer cells are differentiating from normal cells. Aggressive cancer cells are bad cancer cells. A high Gleason is one of the worst indicators you can have and it's scored out of ten.

The sevens or eights the other doctors had given me were plenty bad enough, the number nine dripped like poison through my veins. It was the worst I'd felt at any moment in my life, and it was a while before I noticed Doctor Knife looking at me like it was my turn to talk.

"Nine?" I said. "A Gleason of nine?"

"Exactly," he replied. "Any questions?"

I opened my mouth, wondering where to start.

"Well," I said, "I did wonder about chemotherapy . . ."

Doctor Knife began scribbling on a little pad.

"You'd be perfect for study 16X 98 hut-hut starting in June," he said, "And 99G after that, you would be a good candidate for this study of high risk patients, ideal really, a classic profile, penobium this and hydrocortase that . . . "

He reeled off numbers and chemicals, telling me how great it was that my cancer was so bad because of all the studies for which I would qualify.

"June," I said, interrupting, "Did you say June?"

"Yes," he said.

"But this is December."

"Yes?"

I had to count on my fingers to do the math.

"But June is six months away," I said. "I don't want to wait that long to begin primary treatment. Is that what you're recommending to me, that I wait six more months?"

Doctor Knife looked at me, his watch, then me again.

"Well, no," he said. "Of course not."

It seemed he was pushing the idea of chemotherapy, but everything I'd read said chemotherapy was ineffective against prostate cancer. I asked about chemo because I wanted to know why it didn't work, not because I wanted to do it.

"I just asked about chemo," I said, "Because maybe, in case, there was some new wonder drug on the market . . ."

Doctor Knife positively beamed.

"A wonder drug," he said. "Wouldn't that be nice."

He tapped his chin with his silver pen thinking out loud.

"Perhaps then," he said, "Let me see, study 5050 84 20 starts in March, surgery combined with penobium, interesting prospects there . . ."

He went on for a while and then shook my hand.

"Well, then," he said. "Any questions?"

I was so tired, it was hard to concentrate.

"You're leaving?" I said.

He turned around, his hand on the doorknob.

"Talk to the secretary on your way out," he said jovially, full of holiday spirit. "She'll schedule your next appointment."

The door was open and he was stepping through it.

"Wait. Please. Wait."

It was all I could get out, and that in a choked whisper.

Maybe Doctor Knife was late for surgery. Or maybe he had to go watch his kid sing "Rudolph the Red-nosed Reindeer" at the school Christmas pageant. Either way, his mind had moved on. Doctor Knife's clear eyes were surprised as he turned around, like he'd already forgotten I was there.

"Yes?" he said.

Whatever else, I wasn't waiting any longer to take action. This cancer had all the head start it was getting. I was going with my gut. I was going to hit this cancer where it lived.

"Before you go," I said. "At least write me a prescription. I want to start the hormone treatment."

Doctor Knife retrieved his silver pen from his pocket.

"Hm-m-m. yes, very good," he said, "The hormone bias would qualify you nicely for . . ."

Doctor Knife rambled on as he wrote the prescription but my brain had totally shut down. It was all I could do not to curl up in the fetal position on the crinkly white paper on top of the examination table and suck my thumb.

"Thanks for coming," said Doctor Knife.

The gun-metal grey door swung shut behind him. I'd arrived thinking that I could be talked into surgery, I left thinking all hope was gone. A Gleason of nine.

Why did he have to tell me that?

I'd waited three weeks to talk to Doctor Knife. I'd counted on him so much, but all that happened was the cancer gained ground and I lost money. It cost me a thousand dollars just traveling to see Doctor Knife, and I sure as hell wasn't spending another thousand to repeat the experience, which meant I still didn't have a doctor.

A good, smart doctor is the biggest and most important brick in your wall against cancer. On the other hand, you have to decide for yourself. It bothered me that I'd started my treatment without a doctor, but it still seemed like the right thing to do.

Having ruled out surgery once and for all, some form of radiation therapy remained my best hope for a cure. Nothing I'd read said that a couple months of hormone therapy prior to radiation was a bad idea, there were even a couple of studies showing that two to six months of hormone therapy prior to radiation had slightly improved survival rates.

By depriving my body of testosterone, at least I'd bought myself some time. The way I saw it, you had to give the hormone treatment time to work. You had to let that cancer shrivel, and when it was weak, you had to bring in the nukes. What I needed was not an expert in surgery, but an expert in radiation.

I checked around. Doctor Seed's name in Seattle kept coming up, so I made an appointment. This time it was a five week wait, but having started hormone therapy, at least I was doing something. The battle had been joined.

Think about it.

So far the doctors have given you, maybe, a couple of years. But right now, you still feel pretty good. The hormone deprivation therapy is nothing you can't live with. A couple of hot flashes, a few night sweats, no big deal.

What would you do?

I did what I always do. I rounded up some friends and went fishing. The great beauty of fly-fishing is that you can lose yourself in the process, and if your mind is happy, it has to be good for your body.

After I left Toussaint, the road was so dry that each of my steps left a puff of white dust. The echoing whack of the cutlass was still audible as I crested the top of the hill above Half-Moon Harbor. The flat limestone shelf is the tallest point on the whole island of Redcoat Key, forty-two feet above sea level, and below you the Bight of Old MacTavish fans out in all its glory.

The bight is a semicircle of white sand and olive sea grass a couple of miles across, with a channeled maze of green mangrove swamps to the left and blue open ocean to the right. Near the mangroves the water can be up to your chest at high tide, six hours later you'll be standing on dry ground at the bottom of the low, surrounded by acre upon acre of prime bonefish feeding flats that call like hot lovers.

To access the bight from the top of the hill you continue down the main road then take the first right. There had always been a metal gate at the intersection but this was the first time I'd seen it locked. The "No Trespassing" sign was also new since yesterday; maybe they could have stopped me with a gun.

Then again, maybe not.

The road past the gate is narrow, a one-lane swath through the mangrove, and overhead the vegetation grows back together so it's like walking through a cool green tunnel. Lizards scuttle in the duff of dry leaves littering the jungle floor, and I'd stopped to watch a spider spin a web when a whiff of exhaust was preceded by the whine of an engine.

There are two kinds of vehicles in the islands, new and barely running. The Toyota 4Runner that came around the corner and stopped beside me was factory new with tinted windows. The driver—lest his air-conditioning escape—rolled his window down about an inch, and then put his lips up to the slit.

"What are you doing here?" he said. "Didn't you see the 'No Trespassing' sign?"

The window was tinted dark enough you couldn't really see inside, the lips at the slit were red and collagen full.

"The dinghy is broken," I said. "So today I have to walk into the bight."

The lips were replaced at the slit with grey eyes above the tanned beak of a pointed nose, eyes that didn't look like they gave a damn my dinghy was broken.

"This is a private road," he said. "No Trespassing."

"I'm staying with Tiny," I continued, "For years we've always walked this . . . "

The eyebrows lifted and the lips came back, the driver was smiling.

"Tiny," he said. "The magic word. Have fun."

The Toyota was already moving as the slit in the window closed shut. A bend in the green tunnel swallowed the vehicle but the carbon stink of exhaust lingered until I hit the driveway that leads down to Delirious Dave's. Dave's high boxy house is right on the bight, and as soon as you turn left at the rotted hulk of a boat in his yard, you're fishing.

Past Dave's the shore curves to the west along a flat of solid turtle grass that ends at a sandy coconut palm covered spit, and just past the sand spit you come to a weathered cone of conch shells piled as high as a man in a boat could reach. On a desert island conch is food you can always find, in the old days it's what kept people alive. Tradition was that after you cut out the meat you piled up the empty shells, and that conch monument is all that's left of Old Man MacTavish.

The hurricanes have taken everything else, even the foundation to his house. From the conch pile it's a half-mile of hopping down a low ridge of sharp grey limestone to a narrow cut in the rock that drains a hundred acres of salt flat and is the mouth of O'Brien's Creek.

O'Brien's isn't a creek in the traditional midwestern sense. It's a creek because it flows with the changing of every tide, and over the centuries the mouth to O'Brien's Creek has been scoured out into a hole about the size of a school bus.

The hole is deep enough that the water is emerald blue, and so clear that red starfish and purple brain coral shine up from the bottom. The bonefishing wouldn't get good until the bottom fell out of the tide in another hour or two, so I was standing at the edge of the cut, killing time casting weighted flies to the jacks and snapper that live in the coral, when a four foot black tip shark wiggled in out of the bight.

This made me think of, what else, cancer.

It's never far from your mind.

Sharks don't get cancer. Inject them with a live tumor, or subject them to powerful carcinogens, and sharks still don't get cancer. Sharks don't get infections or heart disease either. Nobody knows why, but I was thinking maybe it was because sharks have been around for over 400 million years.

Sharks were there almost from the beginning as multicellular life was evolving on this planet, and developed immune responses accordingly. If they were resistant to the old diseases, then it makes sense they would be resistant to the new diseases, because all the new diseases had to come from the old diseases. Maybe the immune systems of sharks are able to attack disease at its evolutionary core.

Resistance to disease is a good trick but sharks have a better one. Smatterings of jelly-filled sensory pores on a shark's snout are endowed with the ability to detect the low frequency electromagnetic waves that are the energy of life itself.

It's called bioelectricity, and is produced by chemical interactions in the cells of every living creature. Bioelectric fields are weak, but sharks can register and respond to the tiny amount of current produced in sea water by a flashlight battery hooked up to electrodes a thousand miles apart. A shark can find a crab buried in the sand merely by the energy that crab emits.

I grew up watching a television show called the Adams Family. In this show, bald Uncle Fester used to light up a light bulb by sticking it in his mouth. It turns out this wasn't so far-fetched after all. Recent research shows that the human brain generates enough electricity to light a twenty-five watt bulb.

The brain works by electrochemical ionic transfers from one neuron to the next. Every time a neuron fires, it generates about one-tenth of a volt of electricity, and once a neuron fires, the lingering chemical trace makes it that much easier for that particular neuron to fire again. It's no wonder the same thoughts keep running around in our brains.

Cancer.

As I watched that shark weaving back and forth tasting the currents for food, I was thinking how dogs routinely sniff out bombs that scientific instruments can't detect. Most western doctors dismiss the idea of energy fields that affect the health of your body, but just because science can't measure this halo of energy doesn't mean it isn't there.

Maybe along with the knack to sense the bioelectricity of other organisms sharks are able to manage their own energy. Maybe that's why sharks don't get cancer, because they're able to keep their energy channels properly aligned. If I could get my energy flowing, would it help cure my cancer?

The way I saw it, it couldn't hurt.

I'd been programmed since I was a kid to think of anything that wasn't prescribed by the American Medical Association as quackery, but that shark had me thinking acupuncture. That shark had me thinking naturopaths. Strengthening my immune system made all the sense in the world to me as I stood at the edge of the ocean, open stink box in hand.

The tide had fallen far enough to drain the mangroves and big bonefish singles and doubles were flushing from the dry pasture of newly exposed roots. Waiting with the clear plastic stink box, I flicked a chunk of mashed fiddler crab with my forefinger off to the side, selected a juicy gold Charlie with a translucent brown beard, and tied the inch long fly to the end of my line. It was amazing.

I caught the first two bonefish I cast to, both about seven pounds. The third fish followed but didn't eat, so I tied on a fly fresh from the stink box and caught the next two bonefish, the second of which I taped at twenty-six inches.

Four for five was far and away the best I'd ever done in the Bight of Old MacTavish. Usually it was more like one for ten. Or zero for ten. The stink box was an unadulterated success.

And then I saw him.

A twenty-six-inch bonefish is pushing ten pounds; a thirty inch fish is fifteen pounds and counting. The biggest bonefish don't get so much longer as they do thicker, and the fish I saw wallowing a hundred feet away in the marl was as fat as a chromed pig. The pointed tail on the bonefish stuck up twelve silver inches; the dorsal fin slapped from side to side with the vigor of an excavation as it dug with its whole body into the soft bottom, creating a mushroom cloud of white mud in the clear running water.

The mud was about the size of a dinner table. Every minute or so the bonefish slithered out of the mud and into the clear water, then quickly circled back into the mud from the down-current edge to feast on the tasty treats that had been stirred up in the opaque white soup.

The fish appeared to be totally absorbed in gorging with reckless abandon, but he wasn't. He knew I was there. With every step I took, the soft muck sucked at my flats booties.

Slurp, slurp, slurp.

The inner ear of a bonefish picks up low, nearby sounds, but they also have a gas bladder that hears higher sounds from further away. Each step I took started in a low slurp and ended in a high pop as my foot pulled free of the mud, and that bonefish knew exactly where I was.

I'd move, he'd move. I'd stop, he'd stop.

So I tried a blitzkrieg, several quick steps in a row.

Slurpity, slurpity, slurpity, slurp.

Slogging is hard work and sweat burns in your eyes. Just when you're getting up some momentum you invariably hit a deeper pocket of mud and your leg sinks in up to the knee. Your arms circle wildly backwards as you try to keep your balance. If you fell over you might drown, because now that you've stopped, both feet are rooted in the soft bottom.

You look up.

"Son of a bitch!"

But you aren't cursing the fish. You're cursing the doctor flies, oversized electric blue insects that favor the lower leg, have scalpels for teeth, and take away so much meat they have trouble flying under the load. They are also relentless. When a doctor fly comes in you'll be slapping it away about every fourth step until it feeds or you kill it, whichever comes first.

Slurp, slurp, slurp, SLAP!

Slurp, slurp, slurp, SLAP!

Mostly there is the pain of bites but occasionally there is the crunch of exoskeleton beneath your palm. It's so satisfying, it keeps you going. By moving only when the fish was actively engaged in wallowing I managed to get closer, but only within seventy or eighty feet.

Eighty feet is a long cast but I had the wind behind me.

Every presentation wasn't perfect, but some of them were. Some of my casts weren't even close, but some of them seemed plenty good enough, and a couple of times the fly landed lightly on the nose of the fish just as it turned back into the mud to feed.

I couldn't do any better. I tried different flies fresh from the stink box with increasing desperation; the fish ignored every presentation as we followed the falling tide toward the blue water cut. Skittering charcoal clouds had just covered the sun when the last vertebrae before my brain tingled with that distinctive little shiver I've learned not to ignore.

I turned to look and sucked in a breath of salt air.

"Uh-oh," I said.

A big bull shark was coming in from behind, and right from the get-go this shark exhibited peculiar behavior. Mostly sharks on the flats meander and backtrack, like bears feeding in the woods, following their noses toward food.

Sharks can detect seaborne chemicals on the level of parts per billion, and each of their nostrils is wired to send a distinct signal to the brain. A shark following a scent turns its head back and forth, wandering to and fro as it swims. Sharks are rarely deliberate, and this fish was swimming me down in a dead bead.

I splashed a hard cast on the shark's head, and then yanked the line up. The sound of the line ripping off the water runs off most fish, but most fish aren't bull sharks.

There was an irony here, like Mother Nature has a sense of humor. I'd begun treatment to deny my body of testosterone, while bull sharks have the highest levels of testosterone of any creature on the planet. It fuels their aggressive nature, and the bull shark continued in an unerring course for the brown flats booties containing the only two ankles I have in this world.

I slapped the water with the rod and hit the triangular dorsal fin as the shark lunged forward. The shark was three feet away and still coming when I stomped the bottom in front of his broad flat snout.

The shark turned, but only for an instant, and then showed his lighter underbelly as he twisted back on my legs. At times like this there's no time to think. The parasympathetic nervous system cuts the brain out of the loop and takes immediate emergency action. The brain doesn't come up with the ideas, but it's the first to know what happened.

"*Caramba*! You just stepped on the head of a shark!"

I saw it with my own eyes.

It didn't seem possible, but when I looked down, there was my foot, balanced between the distinctively tiny bull shark eyes. My brain was back in business and I remember thinking:

"Give it to him good."

I ground down on that shark, mashing his face into the sand with all my weight. The shark had turned away and then back so quickly it was curled nearly in a circle. The shark had stretched so far that it was momentarily without power to its long swept-back tail.

For a split second of cold clear eternity, I had that beast pinned. I was a fast-forward man in a slow-motion world, but I'd been there before. The fabric of reality is never laid bare for long. I knew the tail of that shark was going to sweep back with a ferocious power, and when it did, I was ready.

The bull shark twisted into a sine wave of thick muscle that launched me like a bottle rocket. The soles of my boots cleared the water, but I came down on my feet. The fish had finally had enough and wiggled off in a blur through the deep blue cut, I bolted for the shallows.

Even behind sunglasses my pupils were dilated to the point the sun hurt my eyes. The single-minded persistence of the shark had been far too evocative of the single-minded persistence of the gypsy death moth the night before.

Could it be the two events were connected?

Was some crazy fish God after my ass?

Had I done something to deserve this?

A great thing about having a brain is that you can shape your own beliefs. It's the only way to explain how Catholics, Muslims, Hindus, Mormons, Jews, Baptists and Buddhists can all be right at the same time. If a God was after me there wasn't much I could do about it, so I went with science, the only religion you can prove.

On my legs, I counted thirteen doctor fly bites, a couple of which still visibly trickled blood. It wasn't much blood, but it could have been enough to pull in a shark. There was a logical explanation. I'd been a good boy.

Crazy fish Gods weren't coming for me yet.

It wasn't like I was praying, but it was a long ways to the Sea Horse. The thing I wanted most in the world was not to have to walk back. I watched some orange legged oyster catchers stalking the puddles as the flat dried up on the falling tide, and wasn't sure what to think as the full-throttle whine of a small outboard motor got louder and louder.

The sound of the motor came right at me, the same as the shark. I don't know what I expected to see when the boat came around the corner but it wasn't Tiny in the back of the rubber dinghy scooting along on plane.

"Ahoy there," shouted Tiny, waving a meaty arm.

"Ahoy there," I shouted, waving back.

Tiny killed the engine and before the dinghy even sagged to a stop he had the cooler open and was holding a bottle of ice cold Corona up to the sun between the clouds.

"How's that?" he said.

What do you say? Some things you just can't explain.

"You have no idea," I replied.

I sloshed through the mud to the dinghy in the channel. The water was only calf deep but I still kept looking over my shoulder for sharks as I climbed into the boat. The soft, warm rubber tube was as comfortable as any pillow, and there wasn't a gypsy death moth in sight.

"The dinghy never looked so good," I said. "How did you get it running?"

Tiny yanked on the rope and the motor started right up.

"It wasn't but five minutes after you left this morning," he said, "That T. Rex pulled into port after crossing over in Deep Sea Sally from the mainland. And down in the hold he had a dinghy pump, brand new, still in the box."

T. Rex is named for the dinosaur. Even pushing sixty he's still as tough as they come. T. Rex cleans up other people's messes, for a price, but he won't take just any job. He has to believe in what he's doing.

"T. Rex is here?" I said. "That's great."

"Yah, mon," said Tiny, "And he's just itching to catch-up some fish. When he heard you mountain men were down here, he said he'd take y'all out this afternoon in Deep Sea Sally."

Deep Sea Sally is T. Rex's boat, a forty-foot sportfisher with a flying bridge and outriggers and all the trimmings. A boat like that, it's a thousand a day easy if you're going to hire it out.

"That's awful nice of T. Rex," I said.

"Damn right it is," said Tiny.

Tiny idled us out toward deeper water, then opened up the throttle. It's tough to talk over the roar of the outboard, but I didn't want to talk anyway. I just wanted to sit.

It's a ten minute dinghy run across the open bight from O'Brien's Creek to the White Sand Flat. Bean and Montana were waiting by Lone Tree Island, a couple hundred yards of shallow water away. We idled down to creep further across the flat. The propeller stirred up a trail of grey sand in the green water behind us, and a Doctor Fly attacked as soon as we slowed down.

I slapped twice and missed. The big blue fly zigged and zagged in errant circles above the dinghy before coming in low over the cooler and landing on Tiny's sweaty brown leg.

He killed it on the first try.

"You're hired," I said. "Get all the rest of them too."

Tiny held up the fly and pointed at the wings.

"The secret to killing a Stinging Doctor is to hit behind them," he said. "Stinging doctor flies is one of the few insects actually able to fly backwards, you want to swing where they're going and not where they . . . "

Tiny broke off as Bean and Montana sloshed within hailing distance.

"Why if it isn't the prodigal fisherman," Tiny shouted, "Returned to the bosom of the dinghy. Well, how did it fare out there today? Did y'all teach them bonefish a lesson?"

Montana's lips are buried deep in his beard. You never see them move, so it's kind of like his deep voice comes from a grizzled speaker covered with untrimmed hair.

"I steel wear zee white steenk of shame," he said, imitating the French accent of the cartoon skunk Pepe LePue.

Montana is a fine fisherman but he hadn't caught a bonefish since we'd arrived. It was like he'd been jinxed as he reached in the cooler for a canned Budweiser.

"Damn, Montana," said Tiny, "What's going on here? Did y'all do something nasty in a past life or what?"

"Probably," said Montana, then he heaved a sigh. "I had two on. Nice fish!" he said loudly, "But they outfoxed me. I couldn't keep them out of the mangroves."

"Bean," said Tiny, "Tell me what you're smiling about."

"One bonefish," said Bean. "And two barracuda. Nice ones, like this."

It was Bean's first saltwater trip and most of the time he was so excited he twitched; now he held up his sunburned arms so his hands were four feet apart.

"Big ones," I said.

"Did they jump?" said Tiny.

Bean laughed at the memory of silver torpedoes skipping through the waves.

"Did they ever," he said. "Montana got one."

Catching barracuda is thirsty work. Montana drank half a beer in one gulp, then wiped his beard with the back of his hand.

"We still going out in Deep Sea Sally?" he said.

Tiny said, "Yah, mon," and squinted as he held a hand up to the sun. "Climb aboard boys," he said. "Time's a-wasting."

Tiny yanked the rope and we putt-putted through the white shallows toward the deeper green water of the bight. The four of us together were over twenty four feet tall and the dinghy is only ten feet long. Including fishing gear, gas tanks, and coolers we were packed in like toes in a sock, and Montana was sitting beside me, squirming like he was trying to get away.

"Did you see many bonefish today?" I asked.

Montana shook his head.

"We weren't seeing many bones," he said, "But we did see a lot of barracuda. So we rigged up with wire tippet and needlefish flies."

"We got into a school of jacks," said Bean. "That was pretty fun for a while."

"And some snapper," said Montana. "It's not like I'm totally skunked."

Then they both looked at me with eyes that said they didn't want to know.

"I got four bonefish," I said. "And I broke my rod."

The dinghy shifted in the water as Bean turned around.

"How'd you break your rod?" he asked.

"Over the back of a bull shark," I said.

Montana's sad brown eyes blinked.

"How come my story is never the best," he said.

"Bull sharks get lots of people," said Tiny. "How big was this one?"

"Bigger than me," I said. "Seven, eight feet long. It came straight for me, never turned; I think it was because I was bleeding from getting bit by doctor flies."

I told them how I'd been casting to the giant watermelon of a bonefish that wouldn't eat despite the stink box, and when I looked over my shoulder there was the shark. It had happened so fast, a trail of blood made sense, and the next thing I knew I was standing on the shark's head grinding it into the sand.

When it comes to the seven seas there isn't much Tiny hasn't done, but even he looked impressed.

"Not bad for a Yankee," he said. "There's lots of people that swims with sharks, but y'all is the first person I ever heard of that dances with sharks."

From near-drownings to falls to avalanches it wasn't the first time I'd almost died, and every time it's taught me something. The truth I remembered that day was that I'd already been lucky to live long enough to die of cancer. If I'd been lucky before, I could get lucky again, and I laughed.

I felt happy for the first time in two months.

"If it's all the same to you," I said, "I'll save the next dance for you."

Bean wagged his finger like a schoolmarm.

"Chumming for sharks with your own blood," he said. "You'll stoop to anything."

Montana had been squirming the whole time on the soft rubber dinghy tube and now he cleared his throat.

"I don't know how to say this," he said, "So I'm just going to say it. Dude: You should change your shirt."

The only person he was looking at was me so I sniffed at my arm-pit. I didn't smell a thing but Montana is no dilettante. For him to comment it must be serious.

"Really?" I said.

"Really," replied Bean and Montana together.

Tiny waxed philosophical as we started across the green bight, shouting over the roar of the motor.

"A man can't smell himself," he said. "He's like a wolf. That's just his smell. He's used to it. The only time a man misses his smell is when it's gone."

That I could smell so bad and not know, I wondered if it was the hormones. If I had mood swings, I wondered if I'd even know when it happened. The hot flashes, on the other hand, were unmistakable, like getting shoved into a sauna.

The hot flashes had been coming one after another since the shark attack, a little worse each time, and the heat didn't let up until we were halfway across the bight. The dinghy was too loaded down with flesh to plane, so it was a smooth twenty-minute ride from the White Sand Flat to the rock point that shelters Half-Moon Harbor.

Depending on the mood of the Atlantic the swells beating on the low rock cliff at the end of the point can be anywhere from four to ten feet high. When you make the turn it's best to catch the face of an oncoming wave, ride it like a banked curve, then goose the motor just enough to surf the breaking froth down into the mouth of Half-Moon Harbor. You follow the deep green channel along a quarter-mile of cliffs, and then the harbor dog legs back hard to the left.

The no-wake zone begins at the bend, and the back half of the harbor was full of sea-going boats now swaying gently at anchor. We weaved slowly through mooring lines running down from sailboats and motor yachts. A lot of these boats were also full time homes, and a salt-bleached couple in matching blue T-shirts tended an extensive garden at the back of a spiffy forty-foot catamaran as we putted past.

"Are those tomato plants?" I said.

"Yah, mon," said Tiny.

"A tomato would taste pretty good out there in the middle of the ocean," said Bean.

"Tough keeping plants alive in all this salt," I said.

"I wonder what they water them with," said Montana.

"Rain," said Tiny and we all looked at the sky.

The clouds were building over the ocean. The pattern of afternoon squalls looked to continue as we approached the rickety dock just down the beach from the Last Pirate's Pub. There were a couple of dozen boats tied up at the dock, and Tiny steered the dinghy in beside Deep Sea Sally, a gleaming white boat about as long as my house.

"OK, Bow Boy," said Tiny. "Jump."

Montana was the designated Bow Boy, a job which entails jumping to the dock with the mooring rope. He had the rope all right, but he didn't jump as the dinghy bumped the dock. He just stood there.

"I forgot," he said.

I took the rope and looped it around a piling.

"What's the matter, Montana?" said Tiny. "Ain't you got none of those back home?"

Montana's hands trembled as he tried to light a cigarette.

"Not like that," he said. "At least not that I know of."

Montana's attention had been diverted by a nicely voluptuous woman scrubbing at some brass fittings two boats down. Tiny waved, the woman stood up.

"Charlene," said Tiny, "I'd like y'all to meet some genuine mountain men."

Charlene was wearing a lime green bikini that had to be custom fitted the way it curved along the curves.

"Mountain men, huh," she said.

A stocky man with a saltwater tan crawled up out of the hold and onto the deck beside Charlene. Tiny pulled down his bifocals so he could see more clearly.

"Catfish," said Tiny. "Is that you?"

"In the flesh," replied the man.

"Damn," said Tiny. "You're looking good. What'd you lose, about fifty pounds?"

Charlene threw down her polishing rag.

"That was from a week in bed with me," she said.

From above there was a huge roar of a voice.

"Sign me up for a month. If you can do that to Catfish in a week, in a month I'll look twenty years old again."

Charlene looked back, all oiled skin.

"T. Rex," she said, "In a month you'd be dead."

T. Rex is muscled like one of those Old Testament angels; the kind that show up when God needs something destroyed, and up above us on the deck of Deep Sea Sally he spread his shoulders like wings.

"All a man can ask," he roared, "Is to die happy."

Charlene picked up her polishing rag and looked bored. "All a girl can ask," she said, "Is to die rich."

Tiny unhooked the plastic gas tank from the outboard motor and set the red plastic rectangle up on the dock.

"Charlene," he said, "Your only problem is that y'all just haven't met the right man yet."

Catfish raised his eyebrows like he was surprised.

"What am I?" he said. "Crab bait?"

T. Rex looked down on us in the dinghy.

"Tiny," said T. Rex, "I was talking with the Last Pirate and he said they've been nabbing the dorado on ballyhoo. *Ergo*, we need some ballyhoo."

The Latin that pops up now and then in T. Rex's speech is something he picked up while employed by a classically educated old-world mafia Don.

"*Ergo?*" said Tiny. "*Ergo* fucking right I got some ballyhoo. It's in the van."

Montana was brought up that you helped out. It's just the way life was on a ranch.

"I'll get it," he said. "I only have one question."

"Yah, Mon?" said Tiny.

"What's ballyhoo?" said Montana.

T. Rex bristled his bushy grey eyebrows.

"I thought you said these guys were fishermen," he said.

"No," said Tiny. "I said they were fly-fishermen."

Bean and Montana helped Tiny ferry gear from the boats to the van and back down the dock that has been beaten by the hurricanes until it twists like a fun-house floor. I bailed the dinghy down to the leaky plywood floor using a scoop made from a plastic milk carton, listening to Charlene and T. Rex chatter as they puttered away on their respective boats.

"So," said Charlene, "Are you going to stay on the island a while this time?"

"It could be quite a while," said T. Rex. "Before I leave I got to get rid of some vultures."

Charlene took a tiny sip at a red straw in a boat drink.

"I have the same problem," she said, "My future ex-husband's lawyers."

"Vultures?" I said. "Really?"

"Really," he said. "But you can bet I'm gonna *quid pro quo* their asses."

T. Rex said he been away a couple months, and in his absence a flock of turkey vultures had taken up residence on the steep peak to his house. The roosting vultures had been doing what vultures do, which is eat carrion and take dumps. Vulture shit is foul nasty shit, and the rains had sluiced the buzzard droppings into the gutters that led to the cistern, therefore spoiling five-thousand gallons of drinking water.

"It sounds dreadful," said Charlene. "How do you clean up a mess like that?"

T. Rex set a case of Clorox on the dock.

"First I'm going to get rid of the vultures," he said. "Then I'm going to have to drain the cistern and bleach it and bleach it and bleach it again."

Guns are illegal in the islands so I just wondered.

"How do you get rid of the vultures?" I asked.

"I'm going to kill as many as I can," said T. Rex. "Plus I got this roll of spike wire from the Fort Lauderdale Parks Department. It's supposed to be effective; they use it to keep pelicans and seagulls from roosting on public docks."

Bean had carried the Clorox to the van, and had been listening as he lugged back a full can of gas.

"How do you kill a vulture?" he asked.

T. Rex made fists of both hands and smiled.

"Slowly," he said.

I grabbed the gas can and went to the motor in the back of the dinghy. I was trying to be helpful by fueling up so we'd be ready to go tomorrow, but Tiny stopped me.

"No, mon," he said. "Always fill your tank up on the dock. If you spill gas in the dinghy that smell is going to be with you all day, not something y'all want stinking up an otherwise fine afternoon on the water."

I unclipped the black rubber hose and handed up the five-gallon gas tank. Montana filled it on the dock, then handed it back down. I clipped the tank back in, climbed up on the dock, and looked around.

Things seemed to be pretty much under control.

"What else?" said Montana.

T. Rex swept his arm at the bow to Deep Sea Sally.

"Climb aboard," he said.

The back of the boat was an open rectangle maybe twelve feet by fourteen feet with a padded fighting chair centered toward the stern. It's where you sit for hours on end to fight fish that might be bigger than you are, and up front the boat split into two levels.

Downstairs, three steep steps dropped to a head high hold containing a big bunk, a tiny bath, a miniature galley, and a couple of portholes. Upstairs, an eight-rung ladder rose to a glassed-in flying bridge where T. Rex sat at the helm. The bridge bristled from behind with a rack of deep-sea rods thick as broomsticks, each rod sporting an identical shiny gold reel.

We all untied lines and Tiny pulled the anchor as T. Rex backed away from the dock. Head out through the cut from Half-Moon Harbor and with binoculars you can still count the coconuts in the palm trees when the sun-washed coral reef drops off in a sheer tectonic cliff to the blackest depths of the ocean.

A mile from land the water is a mile deep, and very deep water so closely situated to very shallow water is a formula that equals fish. Pelagic high-seas tuna and dolfin are a five-minute boat ride from the pub. The engine has barely warmed up and you have a chance at wahoo fast as jaguars and marlin big as motorcycles. The inshore reef shelters grouper, turbot, barracuda and snapper, and that's just for appetizers.

Let's not forget the sharks.

Sharks abound on Redcoat Key, and no matter how hard you try not to think about it, the cancer is always there lurking in the back of your brain like a bad dream.

"You OK?" said Bean.

I'd looked up and saw Bean watching me. I wondered how long I'd been staring at the curly hair on my thin toes as the sweat dripped off my nose.

"Yep," I said. "I'm fine. I was just thinking."

"Good," said Tiny, "Because it's time to think about running out this here line."

He handed me a rod rigged with six feet of wire leader and a chartreuse plug as long as my forearm, then pointed at a thick lever on the open-faced reel.

"Flip this here lever and the spool will release," he continued, "Let out some line now, mind y'all keep your thumb down, don't let it backlash on you now, then flip that clicker button on the top there."

A button and a lever; I thought I could handle that.

"How much line should I let out?" I asked.

"Oh, say two hundred feet, then drop down the outrigger and clip in the line."

I knew I couldn't handle that so I put our best guy on it.

"Montana," I said, "Do you want to come help drop down that outrigger?"

"Sure," he said. "Except what's an outrigger?"

"I forgot," said Tiny. "There ain't no oceans in Montana."

Deep Sea Sally was now lurching on the high blue seas and I leaned against the waist-high molded fiberglass railing as I walked to the back of the boat. The reel held a thousand yards of eighty pound test line, and I marveled at the sort of fish we might catch that would require over a half-mile of backing as I dropped the plug in the water. The giant lure alone was giving me a pretty good fight as I thumbed the release lever. Up at the helm the muscles bunched under the grey T-shirt covering T. Rex's shoulders as he looked down on his crew.

"Ballyhoo," he roared. "Get them ballyhoo rigs out."

Tiny won't take orders except from his wife and shook his fist at T. Rex.

"I only have two arms," he said. "And I can only do so many things at once. Y'all just drive this big damn boat and go find us some fish."

It takes a crew to run a fishing boat and Tiny more than had his hands full as he turned back to Bean and once again went through the basics of open-faced reel operation.

"Keep your thumb on that line," emphasized Tiny, "Don't let it back-spool, no way, no how. You'll get all kinds of tangled. Bean, y'all run this out there to the port side, and I'll be getting after them ballyhoo before T. Rex loses his gravy."

Behind me, Tiny broke the long beak off a skinny ten inch fish that stunk of oil from ten feet away. Tiny then rigged the ballyhoo into a wire harness that came with a metal nose cone, two hooks, and a purple rubber hula skirt.

Oh, shit.

I'd been watching Tiny, which meant I wasn't watching my reel, and I'd turned around to a terribly back-spooled tangle of monofilament. Only one thing to do and I'd blown it; I turned my back hoping nobody would notice.

Fly-fishermen tend to look on bait-fishermen as lower life forms but the outriggers were a complicated scenario involving ropes, pulleys, clips, cables, and twenty foot fiberglass poles that lowered to the sides. The reels had levers, buttons, and star wheels that set drag, warning clicks, and the direction in which the spool would turn.

I knew all these things existed but not precisely where they were. And now that my eyes had gone, I couldn't find them.

Not without my reading glasses.

And I couldn't get my reading glasses, not when my hands were already full. I squinted at a knot the size of a bird's nest on a reel the size of a toaster, wondering where to begin.

"OK," said Montana, "What now?"

Montana already had an outrigger down and a line out.

"All right Montana, way to go now," said Tiny. "Just set that rod-butt right down into one of them holes recessed into the stern, that's it, not bad for a fly-fisherman, only took you two tries. Now clip it in with that cord there, it's an insurance policy if you know what I mean, insurance that some big ass fish don't yank the rod right out of the boat."

I tugged at the tangle, one loose coil at a time, as a boat at least three times the size of Deep Sea Sally raced by us heading for the open ocean. The chrome and white tower on the boat bristled with antennae and stuck up forty feet in the air.

"You see that boat there," said Tiny. "That's a guy trying to fatten up a tiny little dick. That's penis envy, that's all that is."

Tiny has probably fished three hundred days a year for the last thirty years but he was so excited to be going one more time that he just kept right on talking.

"A tower like that just ain't practical. Sure you can see a bit further, if there's time to look around. It's a rough ride up there, like getting cracked at the end of a whip.

"The boat rocks a little, the top of that pole rocks a lot. Even in calm seas you're spending most of your time just holding on. Y'all can imagine what it's like in a storm. A while back I was down to Cozumel and this old Mexican tuna boat limped into shore after a three-day blow.

"They had this tower they'd welded up, must have been forty-feet high, their spotter was up in the crow's nest when they ran into the storm. They couldn't get him down, he was slapped around for the duration, roped in and swinging sixty or eighty feet at a time at the top of that tower. By the time they got that tuna spotter back on deck he'd broke both arms, a wrist and seven ribs."

My tangle finally untangled, I slid the rod into a holder. Montana clipped the line on to an outrigger and ran it out to starboard like he'd been doing it all his life. Tiny was still working on the ballyhoo rig, slicing and stitching at the fish.

Bean said the open-faced reels reminded him of bluegill fishing when he was a kid; he'd run out a feathered lead plug that was two feet long and meant to dive deep for marlin. Now he was leaning back as he stretched, his round belly and red face to the sky.

"What kind of bird is that?" he asked.

High above a black bird with an eight-foot wing span and a slender forked tail cut the blue sky like a feathered cross. Tiny looked up from the ballyhoo, peering over the top of his glasses so he could see far away.

"Frigate bird!" he said.

The flying bridge was roofed and the frigate bird was directly overhead. T. Rex had to stick his big bald head out of the window before he finally saw the bird.

"I got the bird," he said. "Now how about you get those ballyhoo in the water.

Tiny threw his arms up in the air.

"I still only have the same two hands I was born with," he said. "If y'all want the ballyhoo out, then y'all can haul your ass down here and help."

The point of towers is that you can see further along the curve of the ocean, and what you look for are birds. Feeding schools of predator-fish chase bait to the surface in order to trap their dinner against the sky; schools of bait swarming at the surface in turn attract the fish-eating seabirds.

High-flying frigate birds are your eyes in the sky. They're almost always following game fish. We needed to get ready in a hurry and Montana fly-fishermen weren't much use when it came to the speedy deployment of deep-sea tackle. The little kid in me fluttered at the opportunity this presented.

"I can drive," I said.

T. Rex surveyed his beautiful boat that he'd taken two years to build with his own two hands.

"No way," he said.

Bean was still looking up and now he pointed again.

"Hey," he said, "There's another frigate bird."

"Really," I said. "I've driven boats before."

T. Rex was apoplectic at the idea that there were fish in the area and we weren't ready.

"If you break anything . . ." he said.

I took that as a yes and climbed the steel ladder to the roofed-in bridge that was just wide enough for three side-by-side swivel chairs. I squeezed past T. Rex and sat in front of the steering wheel; he gave me a quick run through of the controls.

"You got it?" he roared.

T. Rex is a big man. Up close, his voice hits like you're sitting in front of speakers at a rock concert.

"Red stick, transmission," I said. "Grey stick, throttle. And keep it running at about eight hundred rpms."

From my cushioned chair I surveyed my ocean king-dom and couldn't help but smile. The hull throbbed with the muted power of the diesel engines as T. Rex leapt for the ladder. Halfway down he stopped, his bright blue eyes glaring.

"Don't lose those frigate birds," he warned yet again.

"Aye, aye, captain," I said.

In my chapped brown hands I held a steering wheel as wide as my shoulders. The big round compass showed a heading of north-northwest, and the marine radio squawked with a burst of unintelligible static. I hung my head out the window and saw that the flock of birds had grown.

"Three frigates now," I shouted. "And up ahead, about as far as I can see, some terns just started to dive."

With our best men on the job Deep Sea Sally quickly trailed six lines. Two lines ran long and shallow to the sides off the long outrigger poles. Two lines ran both shorter and deeper off the back corners of the boat. The ballyhoo were deployed on two rods directly off the stern, and the silver fish in their colored skirts were skipping through the sur-face wake only forty to fifty feet behind the boat.

"That lure on the starboard outrigger is weed-fouled," said Tiny. "One of y'all is going to reel that line in and clean off the hooks."

Behind the boat, a lure that should have been div-ing was twirling unnaturally at the surface. Bean and Montana, so eager to help, both leapt at the same time for the rod from opposite directions. They probably wouldn't have run into each other except the boat pitched at exactly the wrong moment.

"Oh, I forgot," said Tiny. "They don't have no oceans in Montana."

"Bait!" I yelled. "Bait!"

A quarter-mile away a white bubbling hole opened in the ocean beneath a flock of diving birds. The black-headed terns emerged from the churning white froth carrying wiggling sardines in their sharp beaks; trying to gain altitude and at the same time avoid the swooping frigate birds that were stealing the bait right out of the tern's mouths. I spun the wheel, cutting a hard right toward the diving birds.

"No!" roared T. Rex.

"You'll foul the lines," said Tiny.

It was simple geometry. They didn't have to tell me twice. Too tight a circle and the lines swinging behind the boat would all converge on a common point. It would be the tangle to end all tangles. T. Rex would have my head on a platter.

"Right," I said. "Gotcha."

I cut a more round-about course, watching the lines behind the boat. The action in the ball of bait was now furious. Seagulls and terns were coming in from every direction, squawking as they swooped in low over the waves.

"A little faster," said T. Rex. "Just bring it up slow and I'll tell you when to stop."

I tapped the grey ball on the throttle lever forward and watched the needle on the tachometer climb from eight hundred revolutions per minute to a thousand.

"Good," said T. Rex. "Keep her right there."

The dual inboard diesels rumbled below deck as we circled around. Maybe I couldn't smell myself but the scents around me had never been as vivid as they'd been the last couple of hours. It seemed like the very sea air itself was full of fish.

"Do you smell that?" I asked. "Like castor oil?"

"Yah, mon," said Tiny, "That's exactly what it is, the smell of that ball of bait."

Montana sniffed at the air.

"I don't smell anything," he said.

"A smoker probably wouldn't," said Tiny. "But it's there. Time was local fishermen would take out a pig with them in the boat, due to the pig's acute sense of smell. A pig can smell the natural fish oils off a ball of bait from miles away. A pig can take you right to the fish, that is if y'all don't mind following a pig."

"Not only that," said T. Rex. "Pigs can smell land. If you get caught in a storm, they can tell the way home."

"Plus," said Montana, "If worst came to worst, I suppose you could always eat the pig."

"Good pig is hard to find," said Tiny. "The last thing y'all want to do is kill your pig."

There's time to let it happen as you approach a ball of bait. There's time to let anticipation build. The excitement was thick and humid as we circled, as palpable as the salt in the air and the splash of surging fish in the churning ball of sardines.

"Steady as she goes," yelled Tiny.

"Bean, you're in the hole," said T. Rex. "If a rod starts to sing, you grab it."

"Dolfin," yelled Tiny. "Here they come."

A half-dozen wakes trailing white rooster tails cut through the green water. Deep Sea Sally was doing ten knots but the dolfin were doing at least twenty-five. A reel clicker went off; it was the rod in the back right corner.

"Fish on," yelled Tiny and T. Rex together.

Some days you troll for hours without anything happening so deep sea reels come with clickers that let you know when a fish is taking out line. The clicks were a solid stream of noise and line spooled off steadily in the wake of the running fish as Bean grabbed the rod with both hands.

"Well don't just stand there," said T. Rex. "Set the hook."

Bean reared back on the rod but all that happened was that the clicker whirred faster. Tiny leaned in and flipped a chrome anti-reverse lever on the side of the giant gold reel.

The reel quit clicking, the fish quit taking line.

"Now you got him on the drag," said Tiny. "Hit him."

Bean yanked back again and this time the hook hit meat. A big and iridescent green fish left the water way behind the boat. Even though I was sitting in the bridge that fish looked like it had jumped as high as my head.

"That's a fine bull dolfin if I ever saw one," said Tiny. "Bean, y'all got your hands full now."

A heartbeat later another clicker went off, this time on one of the ballyhoo rods trailing off the stern. T. Rex swept his arm at the rod like he was inviting Montana to a dance.

"It's all yours," said T. Rex.

Montana is good with tools and made it look easy as he took the rod, flipped the lever, and set the hook. A dolfin as long as my leg jumped directly behind the boat, and that fish was only half the size of the dolfin jumping at the end of Bean's line a quarter-mile of deep blue sea away.

"So, Bean," said Tiny. "Tell me again about them trout. Tell me again about how hard they fight."

As fly-fishermen we'd been defending our trout in cocktail hour conversations, but it's one thing to catch two-foot fish on light tackle; it's another to catch a fish that could pull you overboard. Bean was already sucking wind. Behind us, both dolfin jumped for the sun, and T. Rex pointed his finger up at me like a pistol.

"Neutral," he said. "You'll pull them right off the hook."

The truth is I didn't feel very well. I felt dizzy and blinked the salt out of my eyes before pulling back on the red ball on the transmission lever. The boat should then have been in neutral but instead the engines which had been gently throbbing suddenly blared to full throated life.

T. Rex was so mad his bald head was purple.

"Not the throttle," he roared. "Not the throttle."

I'd been repeating it to myself over and over; red, transmission; grey, throttle; red, transmission; grey, throttle. I was sure I had it right but I panicked. I grabbed the grey ball and yanked it back. The twin diesel engines that had been merely deafening now revved up like a jet airplane taking off.

T. Rex was jumping up and down in rhythm with his flapping lips. Whatever he was screaming I couldn't hear and it was just as well. I was pretty sure T. Rex hurt people for a living and I was also pretty sure I'd just broken his boat.

I was now as confused as I ever get, which is thoroughly. The seat was so wet with sweat I felt like I'd pissed myself. Squishing on the cushion, I pulled back on the red ball. Everybody was flung toward the bow as the boat lunged into reverse.

Red, transmission.

I saw what had happened. I'd put it in neutral all right, but I hadn't cut back the throttle, and without a propeller to push against the engine had raced. It's the same with a car; you let up on the gas when you push in the clutch. All I had to do was cut the throttle and we'd be home free.

I pulled back on the grey ball by mistake; the engines revved to their highest pitch yet. I pushed the grey throttle ball forward where it belonged, and the engines dropped to a blessed murmuring idle. When I finally pushed the red transmission ball forward into neutral Deep Sea Sally rocked quietly in the swell.

All in all, not my best moment.

"I still got mine," said Montana into the sudden silence.

"Me too," grunted Bean.

"Arg-h-h-h," roared T. Rex.

There's a reason men never stop making testosterone. We need it. T. Rex was coming up the ladder two rungs at a time and it felt like a steam engine going off in my brain.

In times of emergency the hypothalamus bypasses the frontal lobes because there's no time to think. The fight-or-flight autonomic nervous system is deployed as quickly as it takes for the hypothalamus to fire a direct nerve link telling the pituitary gland to step on it. The pituitary makes some testosterone, about five percent of the total, but it also signals via another direct nerve link to the testicles, which is where the real work is done.

It's time for a testosterone cocktail.

Emergency juice on the rocks.

It's an electrochemical response as old as life itself, and the signal to shut down the chemical pumps doesn't come until the blood stream registers adequate concentrations of testosterone. When the signal goes out for testosterone, and no testosterone arrives, it's worrisome. So the signal goes out again.

And again. And again and again and again.

Testosterone! Where the hell is the testosterone!

Glands secrete, nerves fire, blood vessels dilate, the heart pounds, body temperature rises. Women experience similar side effects when their bodies quit making estrogen, a drug to which they are as addicted as men are to testosterone. I've since talked with menopausal women who experienced hot flashes severe enough to induce epileptic fits.

I don't think I had a seizure, but I did get so hot I fainted and fell out of my chair and down the ladder. It would have hurt a lot more if I hadn't landed on T. Rex as he was coming up.

"Who's driving this boat anyway?" said Tiny.

"Jeez," said Bean, "This is a big fish."

Everything was black with blue squiggles. I didn't know if my eyes were open or closed, and T. Rex rumbled beneath me as he spoke.

"I'll be dipped in a *habeas corpus*," he said, "The last time anybody took me down was . . . never."

The thump I felt was T. Rex tossing me aside as he stood up. I lay where I'd fallen, not quite able to move. I wasn't unconscious, but neither was I exactly conscious. It was more like I was so hot I was dissolving.

"Damn, mon," said Tiny, "That boy's sizzling like squid on a griddle."

"Wherever you buy your meat," said Montana, "I don't want any."

A hard hand squeezed against my throat.

"The pulse is strong," said T. Rex, "But flaky. And Christ is he hot."

"Dump the cooler on him," advised Montana.

The rolling cans and melting cubes poured down like the north wind. The cold felt good; so very, very good.

"Emptying the beer in the scuppers," said Tiny. "Now that's what I call true love."

I was feeling better by the instant as I opened my eyes. Bean was in the fighting chair and Montana was in the near corner; still fighting their fish. Tiny was bent over Montana fastening him into a leather fighting harness, and all three of them were tossing me quick glances back over their shoulders.

"I'm OK," I whispered.

"What the hell happened?" said Montana.

I could have told them the truth as I lay there with the cooler upside down on my chest but it just didn't seem like the time to bring up cancer. Not when Bean was latched into the fish of a lifetime.

"Blood . . . sugar," I said. "I get . . . hypogly . . . cemic."

Talking was tough but the lie was an easy sell because with two fish on and one man down everybody already had all they could handle. Heavy footsteps reverberated through the deck as T. Rex stomped away and up the stairs.

"Watch out now," said Tiny, "That nobody don't come falling down out of the sky and knock y'all down when you're trying to climb them stairs."

T. Rex just growled.

"All right Montana," said Tiny. "It's time to get to work."

Tiny stood up, leaving Montana strapped into a high leather thong with a padded cup in front. The butt of the rod sits in the padded cup; with one hand on the reel and one hand on the rod you then use your knees and back to lift your fish up out of the ocean three feet at a time.

"That's it Montana," said Tiny. "Pump up, reel down. Lift that fish up, then drop the rod tip and reel in the line you've gained. Pump up, reel down. Show that fish who's boss. Is it y'all, or is it the fish?"

Already Montana's knobby knees were quivering beneath his blue shorts.

"Right now it's a toss-up," he said.

I felt weak but cleansed as I sat up against the shaded wall. It was like a fever had burned through me boiling away the toxins and I concentrated on the cancer shriveling in my groin.

Take that, you son of a bitch.

My only hope was that the cancer would shrink back to an area treatable by radiation. I visualized the cancer as an octopus pulling back its tentacles in response to a hostile environment, and once the octopus was back in its cave, that's when we were bringing in the atomics.

If this cancer thought I was giving up, this cancer was in for a shock. It's tough to embrace a hot flash but I was trying as Tiny leaned on a man-sized gaff watching Bean sweat.

"Montana's got a nice one," Tiny said, "But Bean; y'all got yourself a man-sized fish right there. That's a damn fine bull dolfin if ever there was one; I'll bet he fights pretty near as hard as a big ol' rainbow trout."

Bean just grunted from where he was strapped into the hard slats of the fighting chair that T. Rex had bought up out of an old-time Cuban barbershop. The chair gave Bean a place to sit but not much else. He still had to lift that fish out of the ocean three feet at a time, and the dolfin that jumped behind the boat looked to be a quarter-mile away.

"Don't y'all worry," said Tiny. "Now that we got somebody driving the boat we can back down on these fish, gain back some of that line we lost in all the excitement."

Backing down helped, but it was still fifteen minutes of steady pumping before Montana brought his fish close. The thick rod in his arms was bent into a "U" under the weight and the deck vibrated as the flopping fish beat itself against the hull.

"Easy does it," said Tiny, "Most fish get away at the boat. Just let him run if he wants to. The fish runs, it just means he ain't tired yet. But when y'all can lift him up to me, y'all do it."

Tiny was poised over the gunnels holding the gaff like a spear. The tendons stood out in his stringy neck as Montana leaned back in one final lift. Tiny jabbed for the mouth and lifted with the gaff all in one motion.

"That ain't the way it's done," he said.

"You missed," roared T. Rex.

With meat this close to the table it had everybody on edge and Tiny shook the gaff toward the wheelhouse.

"Just steer the boat," he yelled. "You just steer the boat."

"Here he comes again," grunted Montana.

Tiny jabbed again and this time a three foot chartreuse and yellow rainbow slithered in over the side of the boat. The fish lay still for an instant before it launched into a string of waist high cartwheels atop a furiously flopping tail.

"Careful now," said Tiny. "What we don't want is a broken leg on a mountain man."

Up on the bridge T. Rex was going crazy that he couldn't be everywhere at once.

"Open the fish box," he yelled. "Open the fish box." Since everybody was busy but me I stood up and wobbled over to the fish box, a coffin-sized compartment of reinforced fiberglass recessed down into the deck. The hinged lid was surprisingly heavy as I pulled up on the inset chrome handle and then held the door open from behind.

"Give her some slack now, Montana," said Tiny.

Montana lowered the rod tip and Tiny gave the dolfin a hard kick that sent it sliding across the deck. The fish had glowed like neon as it came aboard but the lights in the fish skin were going out so fast you could see it happen. Scarlet gills flared as the darkening dolfin bounced against the lid and fell into the fish box, the lure still in its mouth.

"Y'all can let loose of that lid now," said Tiny.

I dropped the lid, Tiny high-fived me.

"One in the box," he said. "We're eating tonight."

Tiny unclipped the six foot steel leader from the end of the line, lifted the lid just far enough to kick the leader in the box with the fish, then dropped the lid. Montana slowly straightened up. His thin legs quivered beneath his baggy blue shorts as he lit a cigarette, puffed once, and coughed.

"Should we worry?" he said.

I knew exactly what he meant. That maybe the boat might sink. The deck under our bare feet shook with the death throes as the dolfin beat at the fiberglass hull in a desperate last-gasp attempt to crack open a hole to the ocean.

"About that little minnow?" said T. Rex. "Think what a thousand pound marlin could do."

Tiny turned toward the fighting chair.

"How we doing there Bean?" he said.

Bean was red and swollen and mouth breathing.

"Too close to tell," he spit out through gritted teeth.

Up on the bridge T. Rex smelled blood.

"C'mon girls," he said. "There's a squall coming."

There's something about being called a girl that gets a guy's goat. It's like the worst insult there is and Bean's eyes bulged out over his white beard he was pulling so hard.

"Get him," he gasped. "Get him."

The dolfin was finally at the side of the boat beating away with hollow thumps that dwarfed the puny efforts of the first fish. Tiny plunged the gaff into the flopping and churning green and white froth where fish met ocean.

"Bastard," he said.

Tiny jabbed twice more and missed both times.

"You pussy," roared T. Rex.

In his spare time T. Rex is a professional wire-man, the person responsible for touching the wire leader that counts coup on giant tournament marlin. It's a rich man's sport and big fish can be worth millions of dollars just in side bets. T. Rex hates losing fish. He takes it personal.

"Do I have to come down there and gaff that fish for you?" he said down to Tiny.

It was a straight line too good to resist.

"T. Rex," I said, "If you gaff, I could drive."

"No!" roared everybody except Tiny.

"Got him," said Tiny.

Bean sagged back in the seat as Tiny took the weight of the fish. Tiny lifted with both hands on the metal shaft of the gaff until the blunt head of a giant dolfin showed over the rail hanging by the lip from the sharp curved point. Tiny reset his feet and lifted again, a five foot slash of color plopped to the deck. The surprised fish lay wide-eyed and momentarily quiet before Montana stepped in and kicked it across the deck to the fish box where I was waiting with the lid open and ready to drop.

"Way to go, ladies," said T. Rex.

Bean took off his ball cap and rubbed the grey fringe on his mostly bald head. Even with me standing on top of the fish box the lid occasionally lifted under the impact of particularly violent thumps. What rumbled like a foghorn was T. Rex clearing his throat as he pointed his arm at me.

"Earlier," he said. "When I told you to put it in neutral, I forgot to tell you about the throttle. *Mea culpa.*"

Tiny sounded astounded.

"I never heard you apologize to anyone before," he said.

"I must be mellowing with age," said T. Rex.

He sounded as surprised as Tiny.

With two in the box T. Rex could relax. We all could. Today, we weren't getting skunked. Today, we were bringing home fish. Today, we were manly old men, and Bean hobbled around still bent over in the shape of the chair.

The first squall had just missed us to port but more storm cells were on the way. Lightning flashed in a couple of different places as black cumulonimbus clouds built over the ocean behind us. There was no point in staying out in a storm, we all agreed, not with two in the box and a roof full of vultures.

As soon as we had the lines reeled in T. Rex punched the throttle and Deep Sea Sally lifted onto plane. Montana was helping break down the rods. He'd just cut a limp, used ballyhoo off the hooks, and he shook the broken-nosed bait toward the open mouth to the Bight o' Old MacTavish as we cruised past.

"You bone-feesh," he said in his French accent. "Tomorrow, you are mine."

Five minutes later we were standing on the dock and I was delighted to see the rubber dinghy still held air. We carried gear between the van and the boats until we were done, then Bean lifted his shorts and winced at the blood blister that spread like a cup of spilled purple coffee on the inside of his thigh.

"How did you get that beauty?" said Montana.

"When I first hooked that big dolfin," said Bean, "Before I sat down in the chair, that's when I held the rod butt against my thigh for leverage."

Tiny and T. Rex were carving up the dolfin on a rickety wooden platform that wiggled as they sliced and I thought of the astonishing power of the fish we would soon eat.

"You should put some ice on that bruise," I said.

"And a gin-and-tonic to help kill the pain," said Montana.

Tiny looked up with a long bloody knife in his hand.

"Doctor's orders," he said.

When the fish were filleted we walked the fifty yards to the palm-thatched Last Pirate's Pub. The Last Pirate is said to be descended from Blackbeard himself of a comely Redcoat lass, and the pub is open to the air on all four sides. The coconut leaf roof cants hard to the left atop cutlass-worked poles—just the way the last hurricane left it. Stand back, and the building on the bent poles is so close to falling over that it looks like it's trying to walk away.

Drinks are served on a hodgepodge of salt-washed cabinetry salvaged from sunken ships, and the stools are built high with a foot rest to keep your feet above the biting sand fleas that come out at dusk. The soft white sand floor gets raked every day for cigarette butts, a blessing to anyone who has fallen from their stool, as sailors celebrating their safe return to port are wont to do early and often.

The Last Pirate has decorated his pub with an astonishing array of knickknacks including a full-sized traffic light on the front gable of the open pole building. A green light means he's ready to take your money, a red light means he'll be ready to take your money in a little while. The light was green as we stooped under the low edge of a roof built out of dried coconut leaves, and the gold hoop in his ear swiveled as the Last Pirate turned and smiled.

"Blimey," he said, "If this isn't a crew."

A dozen or fifteen people sat at the horseshoe-shaped bar, and Montana waved his cigarette in a circle that left a ring of smoke in the shade.

"A round for my friends," he said. "Whatever they're having."

"The coldest beer you got," said Tiny, "And a side of ice for my bruised friend."

Tiny put his arm around Bean who was limping a little.

"Rum and Coke," said T. Rex. "A short one. I got chores."

We ordered up and the Last Pirate served the drinks with a smile that showed two gold teeth. We sat in a ragged row at the bar; Tiny and T. Rex to my left, Montana and Bean to the right. I wasn't saying much, just listening as Montana described his frustrating morning in the bight.

"You know what those bonefish remind me of?" he said.

"No," said Bean.

"They remind me of women," said Montana.

Bean adjusted the Ziploc bag full of ice on his thigh.

"Everything reminds you of women," he said.

"No," said Montana, "It's like when I go into a bar, really, really needing to get laid. The girls don't just walk away. They run. Somehow they know. They can sense the desperation. These bonefish are the same way. Somehow they know."

Meanwhile, in my other ear, Tiny and T. Rex debated the fine art of gaffing. You went for either the back or the mouth. The back was a bigger target, but back-gaffed fish flopped off the hook way too often. Tiny was a mouth man all the way.

"Most fish are lost at the boat," he said, "And the reason is not taking your time. Take your time, control the head and y'all control the fish."

"Most fish are lost at the boat," said T. Rex, "But it's from pussyfooting around. You get a shot at that fish, take it."

T. Rex and Tiny knocked back their drinks then stood up to leave because tropical houses require constant maintenance. They both had things to do. On their way past, still arguing, T. Rex clouted me a love tap that left my shoulder numb.

"Glad you're feeling better," he said. "I'd a hated to have to use you for bait out there."

I stared at an oily puddle of beer in a scratched-out hollow on the bar. Bait. Was that all I was good for? The sum of my life felt as inconsequential as it did absurd. Maybe writers mattered once but I'd been born into a world where it was all about money. As happy as I'd been, I was now that sad, and I was taken with the sudden urge to vacuum a dirty carpet.

Or maybe even go scrub a toilet.

What was happening to me?

I don't know how long I stared at that oily puddle of beer but when I looked up empty cans were lining up on the bar. You have to be careful at the pub because drinks aren't cheap and the Last Pirate lets you run a tab. Start talking, you can drop a hundred easy, and Montana's deep voice was booming.

"There was a rabbi, a priest, and a giraffe . . ." he said.

Montana had his back turned and was waving his arms like he was trying to fly, but Bean was looking me in the eye.

"Is something wrong?" he asked.

Of course something was wrong. Why else would I be sitting there crying?

"No," I said, "Nothing's wrong."

And then I walked out.

"You know what's spooky," said Bean, "Is that I've seen that kind of behavior before."

He certainly had. Bean spent his whole life raising two daughters. The insensitive brute.

It's a seven-minute walk on a white limestone road from the pub to the weathered wooden sign at the head of a jungle path that reads "Tiny's Sea Horse." Tiny was leaning on a shovel in the yard, standing beside a shallow hole he'd scratched through the thin soil and into the weathered white rock below.

Beside Tiny, a pick axe leaned against a rusty wheelbarrow. The wheelbarrow was full of bloody water and the filleted-out dolfin carcasses were jutting out over the sides. Somehow, it just wasn't what I expected to see.

"What's with the fish?" I asked.

Sweat poured off Tiny's short pointed nose and splashed down on his naked brown belly.

"Protein for the coconut palms," he said. "A coconut palm will grow twice as fast if you give it a little meat. A fish carcass in the bottom of the hole; ain't hardly nothing better y'all can do for the roots in this hard-ass ground, except to dig a deeper hole."

Tiny used the shovel to point at one waist-high palm after another that he'd been transplanting in the yard.

"That there's a grouper palm, that there's a barracuda palm, that's a ballyhoo palm, leftover bait if you know what I mean, that there's some conch gone sour, and now I'm gonna stick me in a couple a fine old dolfin palms."

The idea of a fish living on in a tree, I really liked that.

"I'll give you a hand," I said.

I took up the pick from against the wheelbarrow, the raised grain in the handle rough against my rowing calluses. The ground was softer than a sidewalk but not by much. Redcoat Key is a solid chunk of limestone, which is basically cement, and Tiny talked a steady stream as he shoveled out the scant chips loosened by my mightiest blows with the pick.

"Yes, sir," he said. "The way real estate is going up, a man with a rental like the Sea Horse would be a damn fool not to give her a face lift. Walking Stick Mike just sold his house for a million two. He told me they was appraising palm trees at a hundred dollars a foot, so I'm planting me a whole damn plantation of coconuts."

"Course, the down side being you gotta put up with the riffraff. What do I have in common with a bunch of millionaires anyway? This island used to be a decent place to live. I'm gonna have to find me a new hideout, that's all there is to it."

I'd been feeling exactly the same way. The first decent road in the history of Redcoat Key had been built three years earlier and civilization had arrived faster than I would have thought possible.

"I know what you mean," I said. "The gate into the bight was locked today."

"Down into Delirious Dave's?" said Tiny.

The ground rang as Tiny stabbed again and again at the hole in the rock with the rounded point of his shovel.

"Goddamn son of a bitch," he said. "Heard me about a place down in Guatemala, place called *Rio Dulce*, it means "Sweet River," I like the sound of some sweet water, next winter I been thinking of sailing my boat . . ."

"Forget it," I interrupted. "I was in *Rio Dulce* last winter looking for tarpon . . . it's fished out."

The air went out of Tiny as he leaned on the shovel.

"Fished out?" he said.

"Guatemala is run by a couple of families," I said. "The rest of the country is poorer than dirt because the Indians don't even have land. The Spanish took the land away and never gave it back. The poor country people have nothing; they've pretty much eaten rural Guatemala right down to the bone.

"But that isn't the worst of it," I said.

"In *Rio Dulce*, in the lake, there's a plant taking over, a plant with a stringy stalk-like celery that can grow up through forty feet of water. The problem is most of the lake is less than forty feet deep. At the surface the plants spread out into giant green lily pads with little white flowers; the whole lake is choked out. It's so thick you can't even run a boat through the stuff."

The air went out of Tiny's chest as his shoulders sagged.

"Goddamn," he said. "Goddamn."

"It's from the sugarcane *haciendas* along the lake shore. The fertilizers they use run off into the lake, the phosphates and nitrates caused the plant bloom."

"The *haciendas*?" said Tiny. "United Banana?"

For decades United Banana generously supported the American politicians who supported the Guatemalan dictators who allowed United Banana to make fortunes on Guatemalan resources in exchange for a small cut. American foreign policy in Guatemala is a wild read;

there's everything from CIA sponsored coups to graft, corruption and civil war.

"*Sí, señor*," I said.

Tiny hummed a few bars of "America the Beautiful,"
then threw down his shovel.

"Screw it," he said. "This hole's as big as it's gonna get."

In a half-hour of pick-and-shovel work we'd managed to
scratch out a couple of meager salt-washed depressions in
the rock. That trees can thrive in such harsh conditions is
a testament to the tenacity of life itself. As a seed, a coconut is a marvel of engineering because it comes with its
own supply of fresh starter water. A coconut is like an egg
in the way it nurtures its young.

Tiny had been transplanting baby trees from the thicket
of palm saplings growing out of the coconut pile under the
adult palms at the edge of the mowed yard. The young
trees were basically a sheaf of high green leaves growing
out of one side of a coconut, and some thin grey roots growing out of the other end.

We dug out the coconuts, taking as much of the spreading root wad as possible. It was sweaty work, and in the
shaded lee of the full-grown palms the biting fleas in the
spiky tropical grass were out in force. I leaned over on the
pick so I could lift a leg and scratch at a welted ankle. Tiny
pointed with his shovel at a white plastic bucket containing a can of bug spray.

"Island aftershave?" he asked.

I looked at the rusty can of insect repellent.

"No thanks," I said, "That deet causes cancer."

There, it was out. I'd said it. I felt so much better.

"So does Wonder Bread," said Tiny.

It threw me for a loop. I didn't know what to say next.

"Yee-hah-ah-ah-ah!"

The yodeling-yell of pure feral delight came from toward the road and was getting closer by the instant. An electric golf cart came around a bend in the driveway so fast the cart nearly tipped over, Bean and Montana hanging off the sides. The cart skidded to a stop with the bumper not quite touching the tree we'd just dug out. The driver was an old man with thin lips, liver spots and round eye goggles.

"Eh," he said.

"Well, hey there, Electric Bill, it's good to see you." said Tiny, "Now tell me what you're so all-fired-up crazy about that you almost ran over my tree."

Electric Bill can afford the souped-up golf cart with the oversized batteries because he owns and operates the big diesel generators that supply Half-Moon Harbor with power. He was born William, but nobody calls him that, not when they get an electric bill every month.

"Ye needna worrit yourself," he said. "I dinna spend good money on this verra fine cart to be smashing it into a tree."

Electric Bill went on for awhile in the rhythmic local singsong of mixed Scottish and Carib. He was talking so fast I didn't get much, but Tiny paid close attention.

"No kidding," he said. "John Paul Jones is here. Did he get a bass player?"

Montana put a hand on his heart.

"John Paul Jones," he said. "At the pub. Just when you think it can't get any better."

Electric Bill pulled a drink in a plastic cup from the cup holder in his golf cart.

"D'ye ken young Crawfish MacTavish?" he said.

"I played with Crawfish a time or three," said Tiny.

Electric Bill looked sadly into his empty cup.

"And I dinna ken how Bongo Bob could keep alone away," he said. "Not with the bonny wee lasses standing three deep at the bar."

Tiny wiggled his eyebrows over his bright blue eyes.

"Who's John Paul Jones?" I asked.

"You never heard of John Paul Jones?" said Montana.

"Twas him what asked after you two special, he did," said Electric Bill.

Montana enthusiastically described John Paul Jones as a famous electric guitar maker who started out in a garage, worked his way up, and now built customized instruments for players on the order of Eric Clapton and Carlos Santana.

I'd never heard of John Paul Jones but that was because I played acoustic music. It was a big part of the reason I came to the Sea Horse in the first place.

Tiny was a musician too, and after a hard day of fishing it was hard to beat making a little music on the deck overlooking the wide Atlantic. There were always a couple of guitars, a mandolin, and a banjo propped up in the house beside the piano and conga drums, and that year I'd brought down my fiddle.

"John Paul's a picker," said Tiny. "Damn good too. Got himself a band back up north. A real rock-and-roller. I played with him and Eddie two years back at the church down to Iroquois Sound. John Paul's good enough to make you better. All the nights I played, that was some of my best leads ever, down in the basement to that church."

Electric Bill put his empty cup back in the holder.

"Aye, then," he said. "Oi'm guessing oi'll be seeing ye."

His golf cart suddenly shot backwards. The crunch of the wheels on the grass was louder than the purr of the electric motor. Two-thirds of the way through a three point turn, when the cart was facing the other way, Electric Bill looked back over his shoulder.

"Aboot seven," he said.

The golf cart ricocheted off between the walls of green creepers, purple flowers, and brown poisonwood that lined the driveway. Bean and Montana pitched in with the trees and fifteen minutes later we were looking at a job well done.

"A dolfin palm," said Tiny. "Now that's what I'm talking about."

The saplings were now part of a grove of twenty or so trees, symmetrically arranged and spaced to let the breeze through when they grew. The three foot high trees each now rested on a mat of cutlass-chopped fish carcass. The white rocky dirt had been scraped back into the holes, and rimmed up into a dike around the perimeters of the coconut-centered root wads.

Bean shook his head as Tiny tipped up the wheelbarrow and soaked the newly transplanted tree roots with bloody water.

"I never knew trees were carnivores," said Bean.

Montana scratched at his ankle and slapped at a fly.

"Like everything else on this island," he said.

There's nothing like physical exercise to perk you up when you're feeling blue. Swinging that pick had been just the tonic the doctor ordered. There was only one thing I could think of that would make me feel better, and I figured nobody would argue with me if I volunteered to go first.

"I'm going to go take a shower," I said.

Montana crossed himself.

"And I'm not even Catholic," he said.

The outdoor shower at the back corner of the Sea Horse is built of staghorn coral, limestone chunks, conch, and glinting glass buoys mortared together into a shoulder high cylinder. Turn the single knob and invigorating water cool from the cistern streams out of an overhead pipe, and there's plenty of room to turn around or even dance as you bathe.

The view is all ocean, sky and jungle and I whistled a fiddle tune as I washed the shampoo out of my hair. Dried brown pine needles stuck to my wrinkled wet feet as I walked across the cracked concrete patio. Down the stairs in my room I went to the duffel bag for a clean shirt, a snappy electric blue Hawaiian number decorated with swimming fish.

If it has to do with food at the Sea Horse, it happens around the peninsula counter with the four high stools on one side and the kitchen on the other. The heart of the kitchen is a four-burner propane stove with a refrigerator to the left and a double sink to the right. Bob Marley was playing on the direct current CD player, and Tiny was at the sink rinsing off fish fillets the size of canoe paddles.

"Yah, mon," he said, "Tonight we're gonna fry us up a ration of dolfin. Ain't much a man can have that you can't cure with a ration of ocean fresh fish."

I rooted through cabinet drawers extruding twenty years of accumulated kitchen gadgets for the top to the blender.

"Plus," I said, "If we're playing music, we shouldn't be drinking on empty stomachs."

"Not at our age," said Bean.

Bean sat at the counter rummaging through a box of flies. I'd told everybody how that morning in O'Brien's Creek the bonefish had seemed to favor the crab-scented flies and Bean was adding a few patterns to his stink box. Montana arrived looking spiffy in a yellow cowboy shirt with rhinestone buttons.

"Howdy fellers," he said.

Bean was limping on his bruised leg as he got up to go take his turn at the outdoor shower, and stumbled when Montana grabbed his shoulder.

"Let this be your warning," said Montana. "The doctor flies are out."

Doctor flies come in low and seem to have the innate ability to sense where you're most vulnerable.

"How bad was it?" I asked.

Montana took his hand off Bean's shoulder to rub gingerly at the jewels in his khaki shorts.

"I think I might have just had a vasectomy," he said.

He winced, we all winced back.

"What really hurt," he said, "Was slapping at it."

Bean hobbled off toward the arched door that leads to the bedrooms at the back of the Sea Horse. Montana opened the freezer and a stink box sealed up in a Ziploc bag slid down in to the open slot as he pulled out a bottle of chilled gin.

"That's a good idea," he said approvingly. "I was wondering what to do with my stink box."

Stink boxes require maintenance. You want the crab to be ripe enough to scent up your flies, but fresh enough you don't mind poking your finger through it. Freezing the stink box at night meant you could get three or four days out of one crab.

Montana began shaking his head as he poured gin in a plastic cup. He kept shaking his head as he dropped in a big Greek olive and several drops of olive juice with the gin; he was still shaking his head as he punched his hands three feet apart every time he said "this far."

"This far . . . ," he said, "Why is it that the bonefish are always . . . this far . . . out of casting range. No matter which direction the wind is blowing, they're always . . . this far . . . too far."

Montana looked up at the ceiling like maybe the answer was there in the spinning ceiling fan.

"How do the bonefish know?" he said beseechingly.

"It's because they swim in schools," said Tiny. "Did y'all miss that day?"

Tiny turned off the reggae and tuned in the marine band radio to the daily weather forecast and message relay service broadcast for the benefit of the ships cruising at sea. The meteorologist, Barometer Ben, lived in Half-Moon Harbor. His messages were relayed in a network between cruisers throughout the Caribbean, and tonight he sounded confused.

Montana put down his hands and picked up his drink.

"Is it my imagination?" he said, "Or does it sound like Barometer Ben is a little loaded tonight?"

"Could well be," replied Tiny. "Ben don't like giving out bad news. Before a big blow he's been known to take a nip, when he has to report a vessel missing at sea you can damn near smell the rum over the radio."

Barometer Ben cleared his throat long and hard like he was gargling into the microphone.

"There's a big front just south," he said, "And even larger fronts coming in off the mainland. Those fronts will collide over Redcoat Key early this evening, and that's the good news. Even though hurricane season is four months away, a low pressure trough with sustained winds of forty-five knots is developing six hundred miles south of Bermuda and coming our way."

There was the sound of breaking glass over the radio.

"As far as the next couple days go, here's all I can tell you. If you're on the water, be prepared for high seas and erratic gale-force wind. If you're safe in harbor, stay there, and if you absolutely must leave, don't be afraid to turn back."

Barometer Ben signed off and Tiny turned off the radio.

"That don't sound encouraging," he said.

It had been windy since we stepped off the plane. Montana had been having trouble casting and he looked stunned as he ate an olive.

"More wind?" he said.

Bean came back in and sat on a stool at the counter, the thin hair on his mostly bald head still wet from the shower.

"Who said more wind?" he said.

"Barometer Ben," I said.

"Better batten down the hatches," said Tiny. "It's gonna be a two T-shirt day tomorrow."

A day when you need two T-shirts instead of one is a cold day in the Bahamas, and Montana sloshed his drink as he sliced the air with his hands held three feet apart.

"This far . . . ," he said.

If you're a fly-fisherman on Redcoat Key the bonefish in the bight are never far from your mind. Bean folded his arms on his chest and scratched at his chin.

"Not many bones on the White Sand Flat today," he said.

Bean and Montana looked at each other.

"No," they agreed.

I was making up a special tartar sauce to go with the fish, and I looked up from the cutting board where I was chopping garlic, onions and cilantro fresh from the herb garden out back .

"There were bonefish all over O'Brien's," I said. "I started seeing them as soon as the tide fell out of the mangroves."

Montana grew up on a ranch and had country politeness drilled into him as a youngster. He's not the kind of guy to step on any toes unless he has to.

"O.K.," he said. "I'm going to cut right to the chase. Is there room for three of us at O'Brien's? Because if there isn't, you were there first. I'm perfectly willing . . ."

"Yah, mon," I said, "Of course there's room."

"And we have the dinghy," said Bean.

We all smiled. Our quality of life had gotten so much better now that we had a boat, however modest.

"We can pole into the upper end at high tide," I said. "We might find them tailing up in the mangroves."

"It's a plan," said Bean.

But Montana wasn't giving up that easy.

"Because if there isn't enough room . . . ," he continued.

Tiny came back in and went straight for the fish in the refrigerator. T. Rex had arrived just in time for dinner, and he plopped down onto a stool beside Bean.

"Did you do any good with the vultures?" I asked.

T. Rex wrung his big hands together like they were around somebody's neck.

"I spent the time fixing a flat tire," he said. "Somebody left a piece of rebar sticking up out the road. I drove over the goddamn thing. When I got out and checked, it was buried in concrete. Now who would do something that stupid?"

"I told them about that," said Tiny. "It's that realtor from up to Nassau. I told them you can't locate a property corner with an iron stake in the middle of the road. I moved it twice already but they keep moving it back."

Tiny used a wooden match to light a burner on the stove, then set a half-inch of oil in a blackened cast-iron skillet above the blue-and-orange flame. There was thunder over the ocean. It was getting dark enough that it was tough to see so I tugged on the frayed kite string that runs the two bare sixty-watt bulbs hanging down from the overhead fan.

"Yes, sir," said Tiny, "All the modern conveniences, if you don't mind paying for it. Electric Bill, he's charging us sixty cents a kilowatt hour, compare that with eight cents back in the States. For the convenience of said experience, if you know what I mean. Truth is I don't know if I can stand it."

The whole time he was talking Tiny was cooking, first pouring Italian bread crumbs onto a plate, then slicing the dolfin into thick fingers. The fish chunks were dipped in the egg, rolled in the bread crumbs, and sizzled as they hit the boiling oil.

"I didn't get that gene," said Montana.

"What gene?" said Bean.

Tiny is doing something all the time. Montana, on the other hand, knows how to rest.

"The anti-couch potato gene," said Montana.

"Your wife wishes you had," said Bean.

Montana's wife married him because she thought she could change him, and he cast a furtive glance over his shoulder, like he was going to be caught having fun.

"Damn that's starting to smell some fine," said Tiny.

He flipped the fish with long tongs, wearing a kitchen mitt to protect his hand from the spit and pop of the boiling oil in the high-sided skillet. Across the counter on their stools T. Rex, Montana and Bean lined up shoulder to shoulder. I put out plates, the tartar sauce I'd made, and stepped aside as Tiny dropped down a platter of hot golden-brown dolfin fingers.

"The only way that fish could be fresher," said Tiny, "Is if it was still alive."

It had been a full day without much food and the sound of conversation quickly became the sound of chewing punctuated with satisfied grunts. Tiny licked the last of the tartar sauce off his fingers then reached for another piece of hot fish.

"Where'd a Yankee learn to make sauce like that?" he said. "That's damn good dip for a fried dolfin."

"There's some secret herbs and spices I got out of your cupboard," I said, "But it's mostly just tofu."

Montana's mouth opened so wide a chunk of fish fell out. "Tofu!" he exclaimed.

Montana grew up in hard-core cow country where even chicken was considered to be a vegetable. He'd probably never been in the same room with tofu before, much less eaten it.

"Communist," he said.

"It's just that tofu is good for cancer," I said. "It's the soy. Flax is good too."

Everybody's mouths stopped chewing.

"Who has cancer?" said Bean.

"I do," I said.

Sometimes washing your hands just isn't good enough and I could see in their eyes what I'd once felt. Their eyes wondered if I should even be cooking the food. They wondered if cancer was catching, like leprosy.

"Prostate cancer," I said.

It turned out to be a good time to talk because everybody's mouth was full. I ran through the worst case scenario; the high-grade and high-volume tumor, the aggressive, undifferentiated cells. The table was quiet as I described how the first doctor recommended surgery and set my odds of survival at 20 percent with a 100 percent chance of imp . . . imp . . ."

Impotence is such a hard word to say.

"All I wanted was a doctor who gave me a chance," I said. "Somebody who thought they could cure me. But everybody I talked to, nobody gave me much of a chance."

They kept chewing; I told them how I traveled a thousand miles to get an expert surgical opinion at a center of excellence. I told them how much I'd been counting on the renowned Doctor Knife for guidance, how he'd arrived ten minutes late for a half-hour appointment, and how he'd then left five minutes early after telling me how great it was that my cancer was so bad because it qualified me for so many studies he could get his name on.

"It was a complete waste of time," I said. "And when I complained, they charged me anyway."

T. Rex's eyes were cold as raw brown oysters.

"That Doctor Knife chaps my ass," he said, "If you want I can talk to somebody."

"Thanks," I said, "But, no."

It had been the absolute nadir of my whole experience, and that's what it had taken to make me realize I had to take charge of my own cure. The things I hadn't learned from Doctor Knife, I had to find out for myself. It was tough talking about this stuff and I was full-blown crying by the time I got to the part where, still without a doctor, I'd begun hormone therapy to block the production of testosterone.

"I had to do something," I said. "They say you have time to decide on a treatment because prostate cancer grows slowly, but I'd already waited seven weeks trying to talk to doctors. I couldn't stand the thought of doing nothing any longer just to talk to more doctors. It seemed like waiting was playing right into the hands of an aggressive cancer. Nothing I'd read said that hormone therapy lowered cure rates, and sometimes it helped. It just made sense to me to try and shrink up the cancer by taking away its nourishment. Prostate cancer feeds on testosterone, so I took away the testosterone."

T. Rex studied me like he was sizing up a meal.

"What about chemotherapy?" he asked.

"Chemo works best on cells that divide rapidly," I said. "That's why it makes your hair fall out, because hair grows so fast. The problem is that prostate cells divide too slowly for chemotherapy to be very effective. And all those chemicals, poisoning not just the cancer but your whole body . . . I don't know . . . maybe as a last resort."

Bean's eyes were moist above his bushy beard.

"This hormone therapy," he said, "Geez . . . how do you go about blocking testosterone?"

"The cheapest way is an orchiectomy," I replied.

"What's that?" said Montana.

T. Rex looked horrified behind his handlebar mustache.

"Not your *orchs*," he said.

Orch must be Latin for balls because that's what they cut off and every guy at the counter looked a little queasy at the verbalization of every man's secret nightmare.

"Castration used to be the only way to block the production of testosterone," I said. "Now there are drugs that do the same thing, except the effect is reversible. Those drugs, that's what I'm taking."

"I heard about them drugs," said Tiny. "Don't they allow y'all to get in touch with your feminine side?"

I put one hand on a hip and the other behind my head then twisted in the classic Marilyn Monroe pose.

"I think it's working," I said. "The side effects of hormone therapy are like male menopause. This afternoon, when I fainted, I'm pretty sure that was a hot flash."

Tiny cupped his hands to his chest and wiggled.

"Does this mean you're going to grow a set of knockers?" he asked.

I talked through the tears, so choked up that it was tight all the way from my tonsils to my collar bones.

"I hope so," I said. "I'm going to charge admission, ten bucks a peek. I have to pay for all this somehow."

Bean looked worried as he wrinkled his red nose.

"Ten dollars to look at a bearded woman with breast hair," he said. "You might want to think this through."

Living with PMS isn't easy and Montana was edgy.

"Does this mean you're going to get bitchy?" he said, "At certain times of the month? I'm not saying it's a bad thing, but I just want to know because . . ."

"When was the last time you vacuumed *under* the chairs!" I snapped.

It was such a passable imitation of his wife that Montana spilled his martini.

"Mood swings," I said. "Water retention. Hot flashes. Bone loss. If it happens to women with menopause, it can happen to me."

"So these hormones," said Tiny, "Do they cure y'all?"

"No," I said. "They buy me time."

It all takes time. There's a bias toward surgery built into the prostate industry. It took me seven weeks of listening to increasingly brilliant surgeons recommending surgery that probably wouldn't work before I finally realized what I'd known all along; surgery just wasn't for me.

Everything I'd learned so far, that was just the beginning of my education. I now had to learn as much about radiation as I'd learned about surgery. As soon as I got off the plane after returning from my visit with Doctor Knife, I sat down at the computer. I logged on to the Internet, searched "High grade prostate cancer radiation cure," and got lucky right off the bat.

The first page of hits included a one-page synopsis of a just published study on high risk prostate cancer patients. Most studies just wrote guys like us off. The numbers were too depressing, but in this study, even the highest risk groups had survival rates above fifty percent.

"Fifty-fifty," said Montana, "That's not so bad. Especially for a guy that dances with sharks."

"Yeah," said Bean, "You beat those odds every day."

I felt exactly the same way. There were only three paragraphs in that synopsis but I'd read them over and over.

"I know," I said. "It was the first ray of hope in the whole process."

Tiny leaned forward on his elbows with his jaw slack like he didn't quite believe it.

"And all those doctors y'all talked to," he said, "None of them told you about this study?"

"No," I said. "I'd been talking to the wrong experts."

The synopsis of the study described a three-pronged treatment regimen including hormone therapy, external radiation, and radioactive seed implants that made utter sense.

The treatment began with two months of testosterone deprivation to shrink the tumor. When the cancer was at its weakest and puniest and most susceptible to radiation, only then would primary treatment begin. The hormone therapy continued for a total of six months, which seemed a manageable amount of time to spend as a man trapped in a woman's body.

Step two of the treatment was external full pelvic radiation of the prostate and adjoining areas including the seminal vesicles and nearby lymph nodes, the first stops on prostate cancer's journey through the body. What you're hoping is that hormone treatment will help control the cancer back to within the boundaries the radiation can reach. There was nothing new about this approach.

The problem is that in order to reach the prostate, external radiation must pass through surrounding tissue. The radiation can only be so intense without damaging the parts you need to keep, and that amount of radiation isn't always sufficient to kill the tough inner core of a prostate tumor. You'll be OK for a year or two, then the cancer comes back, and when it does, the radiation-scarred prostate fills your remaining days with disgusting and painful plumbing problems.

Nobody wants that.

You have to kill that cancer at the core. If your goal is a cure it's an issue that must be addressed, and in this study, step three of the treatment regimen was the implantation of highly radioactive seeds at the source of the tumor. There was nothing new about seed therapy either. It's an outpatient procedure with fewer of the side effects associated with full-blown surgery, but seeds were viewed mostly as an effective treatment for small tumors still contained within the prostate sheath.

Seeds hadn't been used much on aggressive, widespread cancers because the destructive power of radiation dissipates with the cube of the distance. The effects of seeds are intense but localized. If the cancer has spread, the seeds can't get it all.

But that's what the hormones and external radiation are for, to get what the seeds can't. The combination of proven therapies made sense to me. What I needed was a doctor who agreed with me, a process I'd already begun, but there's a limit to how long you can talk about this stuff.

You can only remain impartial for so long, and when the story gets personal again, it gets personal like an emotional landslide. I stood there crying, unable to form another word, and Bean was the first to get up.

"Y'all will find a doctor, mon," said Tiny. "No worries."

"If I was your cancer," said Montana, "I'd be one scared motherfucker. You're going to kill it dead."

"If there's anything I can do," said T. Rex. "All you gotta do is ask."

Bean didn't say a word. His eyes were dripping enough that I don't think he could talk either. Bean was the first to get up, and ten seconds later the five of us were locked into a group hug that weighed well over a thousand pounds and stretched from the stove to the refrigerator.

The hug tensed at the sound of three sharp raps on the sliding-glass doors that lead in from the big deck. Eyes looked everywhere but at each other; throats cleared as we stepped back, our Y chromosomes uncomfortable participating in such an overt display of affection, much less getting caught at it.

"Yah, mon," called Tiny. "Who is it?"

The door slid open and Electric Bill's bulbous nose popped into the crack.

"Och, aye," he said. "Saltin' up a bit, taint she so."

The wind was up from the east, salting us with the stinging spray blown off the top of the waves as they broke against the coral bluff below the house. If it wasn't raining yet it would be soon. Thunder cracked as Electric Bill opened the door just far enough to slide through with a burst of whistling wind.

Tiny smacked his forehead with the butt of his palm.

"John Paul Jones," he said, "I completely forgot."

Electric Bill wiggled all the wattles in his three florid chins as he nodded.

"Are ye mad, mon?" he said. "He said he wilna stay much longer if ye didna soon appear."

"Good crowd?" said T. Rex.

Electric Bill threw his arms wide to indicate the multitudes. One by one, everybody looked at me, like maybe I wasn't up to it or something. I don't know why. It was my prostate that was sick, not my brain.

"We'll be there in five minutes," I said.

I'd always tried (with varying success) to live as if each moment was the most important moment of my life; having cancer had made me better at it. It was the best I'd ever done at not sweating the small stuff, because compared to dying, it's all small stuff.

We put away the food and freshened up our drinks and piled into the beat-up nine-passenger van with the salt-corroded wiring system that is part of your stay at the Sea Horse. Tiny turned on the radiator fan by opening up the hood and hooking the bare end of an insulated copper wire to a screw on the solenoid, the windshield wipers came on all by themselves as Tiny sagged down into the springs of his seat.

"Huh," he said, and fiddled with a knob on the dash.

"You might as well leave them on," said T. Rex.

Every so often a fat raindrop splattered down on the windshield as we drove the dark road lined with green jungle in the dim headlights. I was sitting in back and couldn't see but was thrown forward when Tiny slammed on the brakes as T. Rex yelled: "Look out!"

The van squealed to a stop on worn pads.

"On the high seas," said Tiny, "We call that an obstacle to navigation."

A cross-hatched ditch ran down the middle of the white limestone road like a wet zipper. The ditch was a couple feet deep and exposed a couple of thick black wires. Since morning another set of proud new property owners were hooking up to Electric Bill's power grid. The flat-bottomed ditch had been marked with a palm frond poking up at each end, but the jungle walls lining the narrow road were nothing but palm fronds.

"Might as well post a dangerous beach with a grain of sand," said Tiny. "It's enough to fool the average man, but not enough to warn him off. Look there in the light. Don't that appear to be a pair of boots to y'all?"

I didn't see the feet until one foot kicked. Tiny honked the horn; in the weak glow of the headlights in the thickening rain the battered work boots waved back feebly in reply.

"I know those boots," said T. Rex. "That's Catfish."

We all piled out to see. Catfish, named for a long mustache he waxes back like the barbels on a channel catfish, walked this road every night. There had never been a gaping hole in the darkness before, and he was more confused than hurt.

"Damn," he said, "Somebody put a ditch in the road."

"Don't you hate it when that happens," said Tiny.

Catfish, laying on his back in the bottom of the muddy ditch, held up an aluminum can wrapped in insulating foam.

"Never spilled a drop," he said proudly.

T. Rex gave Catfish a hand up out of the ditch. Back in the van we reversed course, took the low road down to the pub, and came in lights flashing. The coconut telegraph had burned down the wires. The harbor was full and dinghies were tied off four- and-five-deep at the dock. The revelers had come by ocean, and they'd especially come by land.

Shiny rental cars and rusted island trucks were lined up bumper-to-bumper in the sand. We left the van leaking brake fluid half-in and half-out of the road, and stooped out of the quickening drizzle under the thatched roof of the pub.

A man in a white captain's hat, his eyes closed, slumped on his stool at the bar. A rusty car backfired as it stalled to a stop behind us, startling the man awake. The first thing he saw was us carrying our instrument cases.

"Look," he said, "It's AC/DC."

T. Rex looked chagrined.

"They found out about the group hug," he said.

The man in the Captain's hat saluted and fell backward off his stool into a woman with fake round breasts.

"Barometer Bob," she said. "Get the hell off me."

"That's Barometer Bob?" said Bean.

Tiny sniffed at the wind coming in off the harbor.

"Gonna be a storm on the water," he said. "Gonna be a storm at the pub. There's just gonna be a storm tonight."

The thick air trapped under the pointed roof smelled of expensive cologne and cheap sweat as we pushed through the crowd to the raised wooden deck where three guys stood behind some microphones, a couple of amplifiers, and a double set of bone-yellow congas. Tiny went right up to the tall man in the middle and shook his hand.

"John Paul," said Tiny, "Good to see you again."

John Paul Jones had a deep-water tan, perfect white hair, and was lean like a distance runner behind the sunburst guitar hanging off his shoulder.

"A pleasure," he said.

"Hello," I said.

"Och, aye," replied the man on the left leaning on the upright bass.

Crawfish MacTavish had shoulders plenty wide enough to hold up both his electric bass and his rock-hard gut. Bongo Bob was bald with a bobble-head of a wet shiny skull that darted and weaved atop a long skinny neck.

"Like, wow, man," he said.

After that there wasn't much else to say so I took out my fiddle and checked it for tune. I played a couple notes; John Paul Jones played a couple notes. I nodded, he nodded. Tiny played a G chord and fiddled with a couple of strings. Crawfish thumped out a couple of notes. Now we were all nodding.

"Good enough for beach work," said Tiny.

John Paul Jones enunciated each word clearly like you're taught in prep school.

"Have you a particular song in mind?" he asked.

"I been thinking," said Tiny. "About what we can do. Show them our stuff, if you know what I mean." Then he looked over at me. "Sing that Stones song, the one where y'all made up them bonefish words."

Then Tiny looked over at John Paul Jones.

"You know that tune," said Tiny. "You can't always get what you want . . ."

John Paul Jones wore an electric blue shirt covered with bright green parrots that looked crisp even in the humidity as he turned to me.

"Key of D?" he said.

"Och, aye," said Crawfish.

Fat electric guitar notes hovered in the tropical air as John Paul Jones launched into the familiar strum.

"You can't always get what you want . . ."

In a thatched hut full of beach bums, yacht captains, and born-again hippies, the Stones are like old-time folk music. Everybody knows the words, and the crowd sang back.

"But if you try some time . . . You'll get what you nee-eed . . ."

As far as I'm concerned, a sing-along is the best musical fun there is. Singing is best done in an uninhibited manner, and when it comes to removing inhibitions, a cauldron full of Blasters will do the trick every time.

The Blaster, a pub specialty, is mostly five kinds of rum.

There's light rum, dark rum, spiced rum, banana rum, and coconut rum; all that rum is then cut with a splash of guava juice to keep the alcohol from igniting in your hand.

Blasters are mixed five gallons at a time, stored in a round orange drinking cooler, and served over ice with a slice of lime in big plastic cups. Blasters go down like mother's milk and eight beats into the first guitar break the crowd wasn't just singing they were dancing.

John Paul Jones hammered and bent the strings way up the neck in an electric lead that started out country and ended up Jerry Garcia. I closed my eyes and slid and slid and slid my fingers up the fiddle neck until I found the notes. We'd been playing for quite a while when Tiny began hawking away like a ringmaster with a heavy southern-fried accent.

"Live at Last Pirate's Pub," he drawled, "For your viewing pleasure, di-rect from the harem of Saint Gabriel Hisself, one time and one time only, ladies and gentlemen, please welcome the Salt and Pepper Revue!"

Pepper was long and dark, Salt blonde as strawberries in the sun, and the girls looked like they'd filled the hole in their day with a bucket full of Blasters. They wore loose T-shirts and cotton skirts that flashed fancy lingerie as they danced, and Salt and Pepper were seemingly having more fun than their boyfriends, who were pouting on their stools.

"*O! Plus! Perge! Aio! Hui! Hem!*" said T. Rex.

He was holding Salt from behind as she led a conga line.

"What's that mean?" Salt shouted back over her shoulder.

"Oh! More! Go on! Yes! Ooh! Ummm!"

Tiny's flat-picking style sent the jam down the tracks in the direction of Nashville. The conga line snaked in and out of the rain as it looped through the irregularly spaced rough-hewn poles that held up the edges of the pub roof. Everywhere you looked, people were screaming.

A squall burst overhead, it was impossible not to play along with the thunder. Bongo Bob was naked but for a pair of ragged shorts, and the ribs in his skinny chest glistened in the flash of the popping cameras as he beat all hell out of his drums.

When the song finally ended, people went nuts. It was like a riot. Salt and Pepper were arm-in-arm up on the bar, high-kicking a cancan in their flip-flops as T. Rex clapped out the rhythm.

Crawfish sighed with the pleasure of it all.

"The bonny wee lassies lift my kilt, they do," he said.

Tiny was so happy he was pink.

"What the world needs now," he said, "Is some more ass-wiggling music."

John Paul Jones scratched at his smooth-shaven chin.

"I imagine we can manage that," he said.

"Verra good," said Crawfish. "Verra, verra good."

The news of my cancer was out by the time we took a break, and what I found was that women absolutely adored the idea of a man with menopause. Finally, girls had a guy who could understand, and as we stood around Salt and Pepper were consoling me with tiny little girl hugs.

"The hot flashes are bad enough," I said, "But now I'm starting to retain water."

Salt stamped her foot.

"Don't you just hate that," she said. "Do you get it in your ankles? I get it in my ankles."

Pepper looked in a little round makeup mirror as she applied pale pink lipstick.

"I get it in my cheeks," she said. "It makes my face fat."

Pepper puckered her lips, and then stamped her foot.

"Oh, it makes me so mad," she said.

Both girls looked expectantly at me. Since it seemed like I was now officially part of the club, I stamped my foot too.

"I get it in my tummy," I said.

We all stared sadly at my belly.

"Oh, that's the worst," said Salt.

Pepper quickly glanced both ways like she had something to hide.

"Do you ever get the feeling that you need to kill someone?" she said. "I mean you wouldn't, but just the feeling. Do you ever get that?"

"If you do," said Salt, "Make sure there's an insurance policy involved."

"And you have an airtight alibi," I said.

Then we all giggled.

Salt and Pepper squeezed me in the spice sandwich of their flowery girl-smell. It had their preppy-looking boy-friends fuming on their stools, and T. Rex pointed at me.

"You don't have to worry about him," said T. Rex, "He's on hormones. Now me, you gotta worry about."

T. Rex threw back his head and laughed at his own joke as Crawfish walked up to the bar and ordered a beer.

"Oi'll be having some suds, Ellen, if ye please."

Montana raised his head off the bar.

"Suds sounds good," he said.

"Better make it three," said Bean.

Ellen, a stout handsome woman, took the time to rub Crawfish's leathery arm before she went after the drinks.

"Oh, that's so sweet," said Pepper.

"Crawfish and Ellen are married," said Salt confidentially. "Twenty years and three kids."

The drinks came and Salt raised her shot of tequila.

"I'll get this round," she said.

The muscled boyfriend in the blue alligator shirt muttered loudly under his breath. Salt overheard and arched her sun-bleached eyebrows.

"Oh you," she said. "Do not be such a worrywart. I put the drinks on the tab."

You can run a tab at the pub as long as you have an off-shore bank account. The boyfriend was still muttering as Tiny walked over and tapped the hand-stitched alligator on the boyfriend's powder-blue shirt.

"Son," said Tiny, "All I can tell y'all is get used to it. A fine-looking woman like Salt don't come cheap. She deserves the finer things in life."

Salt beamed to be recognized as the deserving woman she knew she was.

"A hundred dollar bill don't go far in here now," continued Tiny. "It's hardly enough money to get yourself in trouble. It's not like the old days. Time was I paid my bar bill in coconuts. Back then I had the only other coconut palms in Half-Moon, and the pub sorely needed ingredients for the Sunday special, coconut battered shrimp. Back in them days coconuts was worth more even than rum."

Pepper had her head back on my shoulder. She was studying the peaked pub ceiling, which is decorated with accumulated decades of tropical bric-a-brac. There are signed T-shirts, carvings, glass buoys, cannon balls, even some bones, and Pepper was pointing to the biggest skull of them all.

"Is that an elephant skull?" she said.

"No, mon," said Tiny. "That there's a boar skull. Big bastard, ain't he. Look at them tusks. It's all black and charcoaled up because it was part of the first pub when it burned down. That was some pub, a lot fancier than this one, part of a big ol' yacht that ran aground on the reef.

"The Last Pirate salvaged the superstructure and put it up on stilts. He lived up top, served drinks down below. He had it all fixed up with what he'd found, killed, or caught on the island; there must have been a good fifty boar heads in the top deck gangway."

"Wow," said Salt. "What happened?"

"To understand what happened," said Tiny, "Y'all have to understand about Crazy Eddie. Eddie was from up to Iroquois Sound and crazy in the medical sense, loco plenty, seeing ghosts, like that, paranormal visitors in his brain. Crazy Eddie was a perfect example of why first cousins shouldn't sleep in the same bed, if y'all know what I mean?"

"So, y'all can see how the Last Pirate was doing the community a favor when he gave Eddie a place to stay.

The Last Pirate was off to a wedding in Jamaica, he was letting Crazy Eddie crash at the pub while he was gone. Put a roof over Eddie's head for a couple weeks is what I'm saying.

"But then, the demons that plagued Crazy Eddie drove him to the point that he decided to perform an exorcism. He'd trap the evil spirits. He'd burn down the pub while the demons were still inside. That would fix them. So when the demons weren't looking Crazy Eddie snuck out the back and tossed a coconut shell full of lit kerosene through the bedroom window.

"And then, Crazy Eddie, he runs off screaming into the jungle. Well, at the time the harbor was full of vessels. The cruisers saw the black column of smoke. The pub was burning down! The pub was burning down!"

Each time he said "burning" Tiny threw his hands up like flames, his blue eyes blazing.

"The cruisers couldn't let the pub burn down, so they pulled a little two-cycle gasoline-powered bilge pump off a sailboat. They were pumping seawater and making some headway on the fire when Crazy Eddie charges out of the jungle swinging an axe and shouts, 'Get out a me way'."

"Then Eddie chopped the pump to pieces. It's tough fighting a crazy guy with an axe when all you have is flip-flops. The cruisers finally subdued Eddie by tying him to a coconut tree but it was too late. The pub had burned to the sand."

Tiny held his hand over his heart.

"Wow!" said Salt.

"Double-wow!" said Pepper.

"What happened to Crazy Eddie?" said Bean.

"He's in a Nassau prison," said Tiny.

Not much bothers T. Rex, but now he shuddered.

"You could turn the space shuttle around in that guy's butt," he said.

John Paul Jones walked over from where he'd been sitting with his entourage.

"I can play a little bit longer," he said, "But I have an early flight out tomorrow."

Crawfish put his shoulders back and marched off ramrod straight into the rainy darkness.

"Hoi'll be just quick hoff to the mangruhs," he said.

When Crawfish returned from peeing in the mangroves we played a couple more songs; you didn't have to be a shark to sense the bioelectricity crackling in the air. In the same way television captures a soul, music sets it free.

Music is the exact opposite of the energy that passes between a couch and its potato. If Einstein got it right, then where there is mass, there is energy; and where there is energy, there are waves.

These waves can be as obvious as ripples on a pond, or as abstract as light cruising the dark void of space on perpendicular fields of electricity and magnetism. Everything in the universe containing mass generates these waves, everything from the smallest photon to the largest galaxy: even people.

Even people.

People with their own characteristic wavelengths of energy. A certain aura of energy constantly interacting with the aura of everything and everyone around them. The nature of health is as fundamental as the laws of physics. It's a theory western medicine can't prove, but maybe science only needs to recalibrate the instruments. Or peer into different corners.

When you think about it, it explains so much.

For example, the nature of waves is to interact with each other. They ebb, peak, flow, and even cancel each other out. It's possible for two equal-but-opposite waves to line up trough to crest and crest to trough so exactly out of phase that where once there was energy, now there is nothing.

We've all known people like that.

We've all had days like that.

Then there are the days when the planets line up and you can do no wrong. You're tuned in. My body buzzed with energy as we played and I was thinking how my cancer must hate that.

My cancer wanted to live and grow in the basement. It wanted nothing to do with the light. I imagined a giant music-filled supernova shining in my belly. I usually play with my eyes closed because I'm distracted enough as it is, and I'd been lost with my thoughts in the brilliant white light of a space jam blues as Bongo Bob pounded out a reggae beat when Tiny's circus-master voice again boomed out over the chords.

"Live from the Salt and Pepper Revue," he shouted, "It's their twin sisters, from the nasty side of the family if you know what I mean. Ladies and gentlemen: let's hear it for Asp and Viper, the Dancing Snake Women."

The furious bellow from the crowd rocked me back on my heels. I opened my eyes and fifty flashbulbs popped at once. Salt and Pepper, the perky little girl-next-door types, had grown up and gotten rooms, the kind you pay for by the hour.

It was the same two girls on the outside, but Asp and Viper weren't leading innocent conga lines through the coconut poles. Asp and Viper were stripping on stage, writhing and teasing, and when they had their shirts off they threw them into the crowd.

"36-C," said Tiny, guessing at fair Viper in her black lace.

"34-duh-duh-D," stuttered Bongo Bob, guessing at dark Asp nestled into a little red number that was so adorable I simply had to have it.

"Don't do it," said my brain.

"Do it," said my hormones.

After all, I wanted to be a snake too.

"You silly thing," said Viper as I slipped out of my shirt.

"44-A," said Asp as she rubbed her hand in ever-widening circles on my chest.

Through it all, John Paul Jones kept it going and Crawfish never missed a beat even though he was having trouble swallowing around the lump in his throat.

"Hoi'll be domned," he exclaimed.

And then, holy of holies, Salt used my electric-blue shirt with the swimming fish and wood buttons to vigorously floss back and forth between her long brown legs as she danced. Tiny spun me around with a paw on my shoulder and sprayed me with Blaster breath.

"Don't y'all ever wash that shirt!" he sputtered. "Ever!"

"Wash it?" I said. "I'm going to eat it."

Asp and Viper frowned in their skimpy brassieres.

That crack about eating it, it was something a guy would say. I wasn't one of the girls anymore. Or was I? At no point in my life had my body craved testosterone more. The signals went out but the chemicals didn't arrive. I felt empty.

Two beautiful girls were rubbing their lace underwear against my naked skin and I felt no desire whatsoever. It was terrifying. The heat came so fast there was only time for a quick convulsion as I toppled face forward into the sand and lay limp as a gutted fish on top of my fiddle. The music trailed off as people gathered around my prostrate body.

"Twice in one day," said Bean. "That can't be good."

"If that's a hot flash," said T. Rex, "It's no wonder my old lady gets cranky."

Asp tilted her head as she studied T. Rex.

"You're married?" she said.

"Twenty seven years," T. Rex said proudly.

It was the weirdest thing, like I was watching from above. Montana lit a cigarette. Asp and Viper put their arms around each other. John Paul Jones took off his guitar. Bean put his hands together and prayed. Tiny put a finger to my throat.

"There's no pulse," he said.

I was laying face down in the sand. I could have heard what was happening, but if it wasn't an out-of-body experience, I don't know how I could have watched what was happening.

It wasn't that I felt like a bubble, but more like I might pop, so I stayed away from the tusks on the boar head as I hovered ten feet above the crowd near a red T-shirt praising marlin fishermen who do it with their gaffs.

As I floated up there in the rafters, it was unclear what would have happened next. It wasn't like there was a bright white light at the end of a tunnel or anything like that.

Mostly it was just more T-shirts.

"We better roll him over," said Tiny.

I watched myself being rolled over, knowing I had a very distinct choice. I could go back to my body, but I didn't have to. I didn't have to live long enough to catch another bonefish.

As soon as I thought about it, I was back in my body. The sand was cool on my shoulders and broken pieces of fiddle were sharp on my back as I lay there, looking up at everybody looking down at me. Tiny shook his head as I opened my eyes.

"Damn, boy," he said. "The way your day's going so far, y'all be lucky to live long enough to die of cancer."

Tiny was exactly right. It's part of what cancer teaches you, that the best you can hope for is to live long enough to die of something else. The knowledge is liberating, because once you understand you can't win, that's when, with each and every moment, you realize you already have.